Augustus Blue and the
Black Opal's Curse

D1496176

Other books by A.S. Mackey

The Edge of Everywhen

Summer of the Frankenbike

Augustus Blue and the
Black Opal's Curse

A.S. Mackey

This book is dedicated to Mr. Bob's Rocks, whose amazing rock and fossil collections have delighted and inspired countless elementary school children.

Table of Contents

Chapter 1 – The Road to Dead Nettle

"Phoebe?" Dad asked from the driver's seat of the old Winnebago. "Would you check the map for me? Don't want to miss my turn!"

Phoebe sat in the passenger seat with a huge map covering her legs, a map worn thin at the creases where it had been folded and refolded and refolded again over the decades. "Dad, I think this map is almost as old as you are!" she said. Phoebe peered closely at the paper, following a skinny red line with her finger as it snaked through a mostly empty space in the center of Nevada. "Dead Nettle; found it. You should see a turn coming up here on the right in a little bit. It's like the only right turn for a gazillion miles." She looked at him and rolled her eyes and added, "You know, you could just use the GPS on your phone."

Dad laughed and said, "And miss out on the fun of teaching you how to read a real map? No way!"

Phoebe's older brother Augustus sat in one of the RV's mid-section seats, peering through his binoculars at the desert terrain. "So what's this assignment in Dead Nettle all about, Dad?" he asked.

"Well, son, there's a few reasons Mr. Bragg hired me," Dad explained. "He dug up a huge opal three months ago, the largest fiery black opal ever found in America. It's already been verified and weighed and measured and all that, and a public exhibition was already planned. But about a month ago he started getting anonymous threats about going public with it. Since I'm a certified gemologist, Mr. Bragg wants me to take part in the exhibition and be there for some professional and moral support." Dad smiled and added, "And he mentioned that he likely needed some spiritual help as well. Apparently he's heard about our last few… encounters."

"Why do you think he's being threatened?" Phoebe asked.

"On it!" Augustus called from the rear. His thumbs flew rapidly on his phone as he searched the internet. "Says here the town of Dead Nettle is where the biggest opal ever found was discovered back in 1917. It's called the Billings Opal. As soon as the opal was taken out of the mine, a string of bad luck and awful coincidences hit the town and several people died. Mr. Billings donated the opal to the Smithsonian pretty quickly afterwards, but the town never really recovered, and rumor was that Dead Nettle was cursed."

"I am one-hundred percent certain there's no such thing as bad luck," Phoebe said with a roll of her eyes. "I want to be a scientist when I grow up, and we scientists know better than to believe in luck."

"You're right about that!" Dad responded. "Good luck or bad luck is just a bunch of hooey. But the Bible is full of stories about curses and their effects on

2

people. Curses are very real, but we serve a God who is bigger than any curse, so there's nothing for us to worry about."

"Right turn ahead!" Phoebe announced, pointing to a rusted metal sign that proclaimed DEAD NETTLE - 21 MILES.

"So apparently Dead Nettle isn't all dead," Augustus said as he continued to scroll through internet sites on his phone. "I found their weekly newspaper online, and just last week someone sent an anonymous letter to the editor about the 'Black Opal's Curse' being alive and well, and that people had better be on the lookout."

Phoebe rolled her eyes again. "Be on the lookout for what? Bigfoot? Aliens?"

Augustus pocketed his phone and resumed his binocular search out the window. "Well, whatever it is, I'm ready for recon as soon as we're hooked up at the campground. I can scout around and let you know if I see anything weird."

Dad nodded. "The KOA is three miles outside of town, so we'll go straight there and get settled before we head over to meet Mr. Bragg."

The Winnebago passed the remnants of a scorched gas station, and then an actual gas station, after which a few modest houses began to appear on each side of the road. The scrubby desert brush gave way to some scraggly trees and a few meager attempts at lawns. Everything green seemed to cling to the dirt for dear life in the scorching March sun. The terrain began to become more mountainous the closer they came to town, with red rocky outcroppings beginning to slope toward the sky.

"Those are cool!" Phoebe breathed as she snapped photos of the scenery with her phone. "Can we hike up one of these while we're here, Dad? I brought my soil kit with me!"

Dad laughed. "Of *course* you did!" he said. "I'm pretty sure we'll have some down time to hike later in the week."

Augustus patted his backpack. "And if we need any scouting after dark, I brought my night vision goggles just in case. And my compass and walkie-talkies, too. Gotta be prepared!"

The homes and businesses began to become more dense, and Augustus thought the terrain looked a little less threatening the closer they came to town. But when they came to a stop at a single blinking traffic light, Augustus swallowed hard as he noticed a sign on the side of the road.

At one time the large wooden sign would have welcomed visitors to Dead Nettle, depicting a smiling family and the brightly painted slogan, *Welcome to Dead Nettle: A Lively Town.* Someone had used crimson-red spray paint to cover one of the words with a single word of their own, and the normally unflappable Augustus Blue went goose-pimply as he read the sign aloud. "A CURSED TOWN."

What have we gotten ourselves into?

Chapter 2 – Sabotage Uncovered

After hooking up the RV at the campground and polishing off a quick lunch of peanut butter and jelly sandwiches, Dad unhooked the Mini-Cooper from the tow bar in back and the three of them drove into Dead Nettle.

"This place is a total dump," Augustus said as they passed several dilapidated houses and boarded-up businesses. "Does this town even have an art gallery for an exhibit?"

"They just have a visitor's center," Dad responded. "Since the town was founded on mining back in the mid-1800's, there's lots of artifacts and tools on display. Mr. Bragg thought it would be the perfect place to have the exhibit."

"What time is our phone call with Mom?" Phoebe asked.

"Six," Dad answered. "She's taking Granny to physical therapy late today, and she's three hours ahead so that'll be nine her time."

Both Phoebe and Augustus set alarms on their phones.

As they drove into town, Augustus noticed a striking Victorian-style house at the top of a steep hill overlooking Dead Nettle. The dark blue house was in immaculate condition, a stark contrast to the decaying homes in the rest of the town. As Augustus stared at it, he got the feeling the house was almost aware, brooding over the town with a cold, menacing presence. He wondered who would live in such a place.

"Here we are!" Dad announced as they pulled into the parking lot.

"It's ..." Augustus tried not to be judgmental. "Small," he said flatly.

"Quaint," Phoebe added.

Dad nodded as he parked the car. "Let's meet Mr. Bragg and then you two can explore around if you like."

"Is this the police station too?" Augustus added, nodding toward a sheriff's cruiser idling near the front door.

"Don't think so," Dad responded. "I wonder what's up?"

The three of them walked into the visitor's center and were greeted with hot, stuffy air instead of the cool air conditioning they were expecting. They could hear raised voices in what looked like an office, so Dad led the kids in that direction.

A bald, pudgy man sporting a sheriff's badge had his arms crossed and was shaking his head firmly as he spoke to another man. "No can do, Mr. Bragg. That doggone curse has killed the electricity and sent us this heat wave on the same day. We need the electricity for the security alarms and cameras, too; not just the air conditioning. I'm afraid your exhibit can't happen."

Phoebe walked right up to the sheriff and stuck out her hand. "Phoebe Keen," she said. "And the hot weather you're experiencing is the result of a dome of high pressure sprawled over the western United States. Curses have nothing to do with it."

The sheriff was taken aback at first, and then burst out laughing a few seconds later. He leaned down and patted Phoebe on the head. "Howdy, squirt!" he said. "I'm Sheriff Longfellow. How old are you?"

Phoebe crossed her arms. "I'm ten years old, but that's irrelevant. You should also know it's a La Niña weather pattern year, so that's another reason it's so hot this spring, not some so-called curse."

The Sheriff looked at Phoebe as if she'd grown a third eyeball. With a patronizing smile he patted her on the head again and said, "Well, little girl, I'm afraid you don't know what you're talking about."

Augustus knew his sister well enough to realize that the sheriff had just made a huge mistake in underestimating Phoebe's knowledge. And her temper. "Hey Feebs! Let's take a look around," he said as he gently pulled her arm. He could see that she was fuming, biting her lip so she didn't say something rude.

Dad stuck out his hand toward Mr. Bragg. "Truman Keen," he said with a smile, offering his hand to the sheriff next. "These are my children, Augustus Blue and Phoebe."

7

The miner was a bearded, wiry fellow with the tanned and weathered skin of a man who spent his life outdoors. "I'm Conrad Bragg," he said with a frown. "After the email I sent, you brought *children* with you?"

Dad nodded. "They travel with me everywhere I go; no exceptions."

Mr. Bragg shrugged and said, "Your decision, I guess. Hope it doesn't come back to bite you."

The sheriff looked sternly at Dad and said. "You allowing your kids to play hooky from school, Mr. Keen? We have truancy laws here."

Augustus stopped himself from rolling his eyes and said, "We're homeschooled. I'm in sixth grade, and my sister is in fifth. We make our own schedule."

The sheriff gave him a forced smile. "Oh; you're one of *those* kinds of families. Maybe you kids can run along and play while the grown-ups talk business. And don't touch any of the artifacts or the glass cases."

Augustus rankled at the sheriff's dismissal, but he didn't want to start off on the wrong foot. "We'll be checking out the display stuff, Dad," he said as he pulled his sister along with him.

Once they were out of earshot, Augustus whispered to his sister. "Just forget about him," he said. "Don't want to stir up any trouble for Dad while we're here, especially from the sheriff."

Phoebe clenched her fists together. "You're right, but he's … insufferable!"

Augustus pulled a walkie from his backpack and passed it to Phoebe. "I don't know what that word

8

means, but don't let him get to you," he said. "Keep this walkie with you while we see what's on display in the cases."

They meandered through the center, peering into locked Lucite boxes housing pick-axes, vintage dynamite blasting caps, ropes, and old sieve pans with rusted screens. "Look at these cool pictures!" Augustus said.

A series of grainy black and white photos filled one of the cases, along with what appeared to be a collection of tattered personal diaries. "Oh, check out Mr. Billings posing with his opal," Phoebe said, pointing to a photo of a smiling man holding a rock. "I thought it'd be bigger."

Sweat began to form on Augustus's brow and the backs of his knees. "Man, it's stuffy in here!"

"Way hotter outside, though," Phoebe responded. "Oh, looks like there's some kind of break room over here."

Augustus and Phoebe wandered into a small room with a counter, sink, fridge, microwave, and a vending machine. "I wish the electricity worked so I could get a cold soda!"

"Me, too!" Phoebe replied as she opened the fridge. "Nothing but some sticky-looking mustard and ketchup packets in here. Gross, it stinks!"

"Wonder where that door leads," Augustus said as he pointed to the far corner of the room where a narrow door stood ajar beside the soda machine.

Augustus pulled his cell phone from his pocket and aimed the flashlight into what at first appeared to be a closet. "Ah, it's the power center for the building," he said as he pulled the door all the way open, making note of the fuse box and the alarm system.

"Whoa!" he whispered as he moved to get a closer look at the fuse box. "Glass fuses! This building must have been built a long time ago if it's still got those."

"Aren't there some missing?" Phoebe asked. "Looks like there's supposed to be six of those fuses, and I only see four."

Augustus nodded. "Looks that way to me, too. But hold on…" He leaned in closer with his flashlight. "Look at that!" he whispered.

"What?" Phoebe asked.

Augustus pulled a pen from his backpack. Careful not to touch anything, he aimed his phone at the fuse box and started recording while using the tip of his pen to point at some of the wires. "What does that look like to you?" he asked.

Phoebe gasped in alarm. "No way! Do you think--"

"Yep," Augustus said. "All of these wires have been cut, clean through. You were right about it not being a curse. This was deliberate."

Augustus quickly stowed his phone and pulled Phoebe out of the closet.

"Something is going on here, and we need to talk to Dad. Alone."

Chapter 3 – The Blackwood Witch

"What's so important that it couldn't wait?" Dad asked, looking between Augustus and Phoebe.

A few minutes earlier Augustus had interrupted the adults-only meeting with their private, "this is a *really* important emergency" family code phrase. He had looked Dad directly in the eye and said simply, "Joshua called, and he said it's important."

Dad had immediately wrapped up his meeting with the sheriff and Mr. Bragg. Without asking any questions, he had followed the kids outside and across the street into Milly's Diner. Thankfully Milly's air conditioning was working, and they relished the cool indoor air.

A gray-haired waitress with dark circles under her eyes came to the table and they all ordered grilled cheese sandwiches, fries, and ice cold lemonade. Once the waitress left, Augustus leaned toward Dad and held up his cell phone. "The electricity in the building wasn't down because of some curse. The wires were cut. Deliberately," he whispered.

As Dad watched the video, his brow furrowed in confusion. Then he sat back and said, "Now, why in the world would the sheriff lie about something like that?"

Augustus looked at Phoebe and shrugged. "Looks like someone definitely doesn't want that new opal exhibit to happen," he suggested.

The waitress brought their lemonades and they took a moment to enjoy a long, refreshing drink. Then Dad looked up at the ceiling and said, "God, we ask for your wisdom in this situation. Give us understanding, and speak to us about our role here in this town full of people that you love very, very much. We ask for your constant protection, and we ask you to trip up the snares of the enemy. Amen."

Augustus and Phoebe both nodded and echoed, "Amen!"

Just then the bell jingled as a boy about Phoebe's age came into the diner. Augustus had seen a school bus drop the boy off just outside moments earlier.

"Hi, Grandma!" said the boy as he dropped his backpack onto the floor and sat on a stool at the counter.

The gray-haired waitress brought him a slice of apple pie and an ice water, then ruffled his hair gently. "How was school?"

The boy shrugged and looked over at Augustus and Phoebe with unabashed curiosity. "Eh, it was fine," he said with a mouth full of pie.

Augustus felt in his belly that he needed to get to know this kid. He called out, "Hey! Want to join us?"

The boy shrugged again, then picked up his pie and water and ambled toward their booth. Dad scooted over so the boy could join them, and their meals arrived a moment later.

"New in town?" the boy asked.

Dad smiled. "Yep! Just visiting for a little while," he said. "I'm Truman Keen, and this is my son Augustus Blue and my daughter Phoebe."

"That's my Grandma Milly over there," the boy said as he thumbed in the direction of the kitchen. "I'm Landon."

"You live here?" Phoebe asked with her mouth full of fries.

"Sorta. Grandma and I live in her camper at the KOA outside of town," Landon replied.

"No way!" Augustus said. "We just hooked up there earlier today. Pretty nice campground."

Landon shrugged and finished off his pie. "It's fine. Better than being homeless, I guess."

Phoebe cut straight to the chase. "So we keep hearing about this curse thing. What's that all about?" she asked.

Landon nodded. "Oh, yeah, it's like, a real thing," he said. "I guess back in 1917 when the Billings Opal – you've heard of that, right?"

Dad, Augustus, and Phoebe all nodded, and Landon continued.

"Anyway, so the opal was dug out of the Blackwood Mine, way up on that rise." He pointed out the window toward a towering, windswept outcropping that seemed to overshadow the town. "Mr. Billings and another guy mined the cave and took the opal, but it turns out it wasn't their land. It

13

belonged to a lady named Merletta Blackwood, and they say she put a curse on the whole town because of it."

Dad chewed thoughtfully, then asked, "Why do people say that? Do you know what happened?"

The gray-haired waitress came over to the table just then. "Couldn't help but overhear," she said with a frown. "I'm Milly, and I can tell you all about it, because my family has been here forever and knows all the stories."

"By all means!" said Dad.

Augustus wondered why the kindly-looking waitress seemed so exhausted.

Milly cleared her throat and recited the legend with theatrical emphasis. "So the very same day that opal was taken out of the mine, the city's three councilmen all died, tragic horrible deaths. First it was Roy Banks. Fell into a well & drowned just after sunset. Not twenty minutes after that, a guy named Willie Hatcher was bit by a Mojave rattlesnake, and was stone cold dead in ten minutes. When the other councilman Fred Brownlee tried to load up the body a few hours later, something spooked his mule and he was kicked in the head." She looked back and forth between Dad and Augustus with eyes wide as saucers as she added, "And every one of their wives said the Blackwood Witch had passed by their door right when it happened. It's all recorded in some of the diaries from back then."

"Who's the Blackwood Witch?" Augustus asked.

14

"That was the townspeople's nickname for Merletta Blackwood, the lady that actually owned the land where the opal was mined," Milly explained.

"Was she actually a witch?" Dad asked. "Or did people just call her that?"

Milly shrugged, and then looked from Augustus to Phoebe to Dad. "The old families here say she was, but I don't know for sure. Either way, you might want to watch your backs while you're here, and watch each other's backs. I'd even suggest you cut your visit short," she warned, her mouth set in a thin line. "Sometimes weird things happen to people who visit and start meddling. Nightmares. Car trouble. Broken bones. I've seen it all."

Just then the door opened and the bell jingled again. "Excuse me," Milly said with a brief nod as she went to wait on a new set of customers.

Dad ate another few fries and said, "Landon, I really appreciate you and your grandmother giving us the backstory of this place. But my children and I follow Jesus, and we believe that he is way more powerful than any curse, so we don't have anything to be afraid of. We'll just plan to enjoy our time here and help out a friend with his exhibit. We might even get some hiking in while we're here."

Landon cocked his head sideways. "Jesus?" he echoed. "So you guys are into that religion stuff, huh? Not my thing, but that's cool for you." He downed the rest of his water, then rose from the table and said, "Homework calls."

Augustus waved. "See you around the KOA!"

15

The Keen's finished the last of their sandwiches and fries. Then Dad gazed up at the towering sandstone outcropping in the near distance. Then he said quietly, "I guess we need to find out who sabotaged the visitor's center, and why."

Augustus gave Phoebe a high five as he said, "Bring it on!"

Chapter 4 – Friend or Foe?

The door to the diner flew open with such force that Augustus was surprised the jangling bell wasn't destroyed. A tall, white-haired woman bustled into the diner with a frown on her face, surveying the patrons currently inside. When she saw the Keen family, her frown was instantly replaced with a smile that seemed a little too wide and very much fake. Augustus decided to withhold judgment until they'd had a chance to talk to her.

She walked toward them with the commanding air of someone used to getting her way, making a beeline for Dad. "Harriet Longfellow," she announced loudly. "You must be Mr. Keen. I wanted to personally welcome you all to Dead Nettle."

Augustus noticed that the angry gleam in the woman's eye didn't match the plastic smile she was wearing. He rose from the booth and stuck out his hand. "Augustus Blue," he said cordially. "That's my dad Truman, and my sister Phoebe."

Harriet's initial confusion was quickly replaced by a saccharin smile as she shook his hand. "Oh, how *cute!*" Looking at Dad she said, "My nephew told me you brought your little ones with you to visit. How sweet that you all travel together."

Augustus sat back down in the booth and Phoebe asked, "Your last name is Longfellow? Like the sheriff?"

Harriet glanced at Phoebe, but then addressed Dad. "Sheriff Longfellow is my nephew, and I'm sure he told you about the unfortunate incident over at the visitor's center."

Dad nodded, and Augustus was glad that Dad chose his words carefully. "Oh, yes, Ma'am," Dad said. "He told us everything they know about the electricity and the heat wave interfering with Mr. Bragg's planned exhibit."

Harriet gave him a satisfied nod. "Exactly. My family has been in Dead Nettle since before that dreadful curse business started. Perhaps you may have noticed my historic home, the big Victorian at the top of the hill?"

Augustus tried to hide his surprise. *So she lives in that creepy blue house?"* he thought. *"Makes perfect sense!"*

Dad shook his head and politely said, "I'm afraid I didn't, actually."

Harriet's surprise was quickly masked with another plastic smile. "No matter. Anyway, as I was saying, my family has been here longer than anyone, and we know not to upset the apple cart, if you know what I mean."

Dad smiled. "Well, not really. Can you tell me more?"

18

Harriet shrugged, and it was all Augustus could do not to roll his eyes at how thick she seemed to lay on the sadness act.

"Well, I'm just *so* sorry you had to drive all this way for nothing," she said. She reached into her purse and pulled out two very large lollipops and passed one each to Augustus and Phoebe.

"I'm sort of the unofficial spokesperson for the town," Harriet said with a smug smile. "Of *course* I want exhibits and the like to take place here, since it's good for our community. I can't tell you how much I had looked forward to Mr. Bragg's exhibit. But when the curse gets all riled up like it has, and unfortunate things start happening, it's just safer for everyone if we just keep to ourselves." She shrugged. "I'm afraid it just can't happen, and I'm glad no one was hurt. *This* time."

Phoebe cocked her head sideways, ignoring her unopened lollipop. "So, you said your family was part of the original Billings Opal discovery," she said. "Is the Billings family still around?"

Harriet seemed to swell with pride as she recounted her story. "My Grandfather Longfellow was Mr. Billings' sole business partner, and he actually helped extract the fiery opal that Mr. Billings had discovered. But Mr. Billings dissolved the partnership the very next day, and the whole Billings family left three days later and never came back; not even to visit. But the Longfellows …" She drew herself up tall and lifted her chin. "We stayed on. Almost single-handedly, my

19

grandparents kept the town of Dead Nettle going, and helped make the town into what it is today."

Augustus wanted to point out to Ms. Longfellow that today the town was dilapidated and far from thriving, but he kept his words to himself.

Milly stopped by, and her eyes grew wide when she saw who was standing next to the Keen's table. "Harriet!" she said after a moment. She swallowed hard, and Augustus noticed Milly's hands were shaking. "How nice of you to drop in," she managed. "Can I get you anything? A cup of coffee? Some pie? On the house, of course."

Harriet waved her off. "No, thank you," she said curtly. "I won't be staying long."

After Milly was out of earshot, Harriet leaned closer to Dad and lowered her voice. "Truth be told, I don't think Mr. Bragg's new discovery is even the real thing."

Dad's eyebrows shot up in surprise. "But it's been verified and authenticated."

Harriet smiled as if she were speaking to an ignorant child. "Oh, anybody can get on the internet and buy a certificate claiming anything is *authentic*," she said, putting air quotes around the last word. "I'm sure it's just a fake, or if it truly is a fiery black opal, it's probably not as large as Mr. Bragg claims it to be." She let out a harsh laugh. "With a name like Bragg, I mean, who would believe him anyway? I really think the poor man is just trying to upstage the Billings Opal, and upstage my family's good name and long-standing reputation. That's probably why these unfortunate circumstances have happened with the visitor's center."

She nodded firmly. "With the curse being alive and well, it's safest for everyone that the show not take place; simple as that."

Dad rose from the booth. "I appreciate you sharing all of that, Ms. Longfellow."

"Oh, please," she said in a syrupy voice as she patted his arm. "Do call me Harriet."

Dad nodded. "Okay. But we plan to continue helping Mr. Bragg get the exhibition set up, despite what everyone is saying."

Harriet's jaw dropped. "You can't be serious!"

Augustus wanted to interrupt and tell the old lady that of course Dad was serious. Once again, he held his tongue, hiding a smile by taking a sip of lemonade.

Dad smiled at the woman tenderly. "You see, Harriet, we don't fear curses. We follow Jesus, and we follow his word that says we can choose not to live in fear, so that's the choice we've made. Simple as that."

Augustus had to cover up a giggle with a fake cough, surprised and impressed that Dad had used the lady's exact words.

All trace of sugary sweetness evaporated from Harriet's face as she looked from Dad to Augustus to Phoebe and back to Dad again, her eyes flashing black with anger. "Well, Mr. Keen, I've met some foolish folks in my day, but none as foolish as you. You've been warned."

She turned on her heel and marched out of the diner.

Chapter 5 – The Power Stone

The next morning after the breakfast cereal dishes were cleaned up, Dad looked at his watch and said. "Let's head out. I'm meeting with Mr. Bragg in twenty minutes at his place," he said.

"Is there an actual hotel in this little town?" Augustus asked as the three of them piled into the car. "I wondered where Mr. Bragg was staying."

Dad opened the car door and was hit with a blast of super-heated air. "Whoa! Didn't think it'd be so hot this early! Let's let it cool down some." He gingerly cranked up the car and turned the air on full blast, then pointed toward the town. "There's a bed and breakfast inn not too far from Milly's Diner."

A short while later Dad knocked on the door of a picturesque little cottage and was greeted by a tiny woman with bright white hair. "Good morning," she said pleasantly. "You must be Mr. Keen. I'm Brenda Conner. Mr. Bragg is in the study; down the hall and to the right. Make yourselves at home."

As they walked down the hallway, Phoebe asked, "Do we get to see the opal, Dad?"

That question was answered when they all entered the study at the end of the hall. Mr. Bragg was standing at the window holding a large stone up to the light and turning it this way and that way. He had a faraway smile on his face.

"She's a beauty, isn't she?" he breathed.

Phoebe walked straight up to Mr. Bragg and said, "Can I hold it? I want to see what all the fuss is about."

Dad passed Phoebe a pair of soft cotton gloves. Even though the adult-sized gloves dwarfed her hands, she dutifully put them on and held her hands open. As Mr. Bragg laid the brilliant stone in her open palms she said, "I read up on these fiery black opals. Did you know they are scarcer than diamonds?"

Mr. Bragg raised his brows with a smile and said, "Sure did! Are you planning to become a gemologist like your dad?"

"Nope," Phoebe replied. She held the opal up to the light and looked closely at the shimmering colors. "But I *am* going to be a scientist when I grow up, and I like to learn about how stuff works. I read that regular opals are fairly common, but the black ones are really rare."

She handed the gem back to Mr. Bragg and said, "I also read that a black opal is highly prized as a power stone for magic rituals. Did you know about that, too?"

Mr. Bragg nodded. "Oh, yes. I mean, I don't care about all that, because my interest is in the hunt of actually finding them, not using them in some mumbo-jumbo ritual sort of thing." He sighed and added, "But now all these threats and constant talk of curses is sort of giving me the willies."

Augustus chimed in. "We heard all about the land belonging to Merletta Blackwood. One of the local kids told us about her."

Dad donned the cotton gloves and examined the opal himself. "That was back in 1917, so surely someone else owns the land now," he said.

Mr. Bragg nodded. "Oh, yes. I would never mine on someone else's land unless I had permission. Ms. Blackwood passed away twenty years ago, leaving no will and no heir. I own a land investment company, and it took about six years going through the courts, but I was finally able to buy her property, so the land is mine now."

Dad passed the stone back to Mr. Bragg and said, "Ownership is a powerful thing."

Mr. Bragg cocked his head sideways and asked, "What do you mean by that?"

"I mean that if you own the land, you have authority over it, both in the natural and in the spiritual," Dad explained.

Mr. Bragg said, "I won't pretend to understand what you just said, Truman. But I'll admit that one of the reasons I asked you to come to Dead Nettle is because people tell me you know about ... spiritual things like this, and I don't." He shrugged and added, "I do believe in God, just to be clear. But I heard from a half-dozen people who were at the Miami gemologists convention last year, and they all told me about how you took on that guy that went off the rails in the middle of the hotel."

Augustus grinned. "You should have seen it! That demon didn't stand a chance."

Mr. Bragg's face paled. "Did you say *demon*? You can't be serious!"

Dad nodded firmly. "Oh, yes. Completely serious. The Bible tells us that they are real, but here in America we've become cynical about the spirit world. If it can't be measured in a test tube or explained by science, we Westerners usually don't believe it. But my children and I have seen it first hand, many times, and the gentleman in Miami was definitely being harassed by a demon."

Augustus could tell Mr. Bragg was having a hard time believing them. "Scout's honor!" he said. "That one was nasty. Smelled like a dead animal."

Phoebe nodded with a disgusted scowl. "It was *really* gross!"

Mr. Bragg looked at the opal in his hand and quietly asked, "So what did you do about that demon, exactly?"

Dad shrugged. "We prayed. We commanded the demon to be quiet and leave, and it had no choice but to obey."

Mr. Bragg's jaw dropped. "That's it? No holy water? No ... I don't know, silver bullets or incense or anything?"

Dad nodded. "That's it. We spoke to the demon and commanded it to go, and when the guy was in his right mind a few minutes later, we talked to him about how he needed a relationship with Jesus. I still keep in touch with him, and he's living a healthy, happy, demon-free life that honors God."

Mr. Bragg cocked his head sideways. "So, do you think that's what we're dealing with here in Dead Nettle? Some demon thing you can yell at and make go away? Surely there's more to it than that."

Augustus took his phone from his pocket. "Can I show him what we discovered yesterday, Dad?"

Dad nodded. "Of course!"

"We haven't told anyone else what we know," said Augustus as he queued up the video of the sabotaged fuse box and played it for Mr. Bragg.

After watching the video, Mr. Bragg began to pace. "Why in the world would someone want to sabotage the exhibit?" he asked. "And the sheriff *had* to have seen those cut wires. The fuse box is the first thing you'd check when the power goes off. It doesn't make any sense!"

Dad nodded. "I agree completely! I'm not pointing fingers, but something fishy is definitely going on."

Augustus crossed his arms and said, "So it looks like the three of us are going to help you get to the bottom of this!"

Mr. Bragg nodded forcefully and said, "Excellent! Now where do we start?"

Chapter 6 – Myths and Legends

Dad suggested that he and the kids should do some more fact-finding legwork, and they agreed to meet up with Mr. Bragg early the next morning to explore the mine together. The Mini-Cooper was running on empty, so they headed to Gilmore's Gas and Tires a few blocks away.

A burly man with oil-stained fingers came out of the gas station as the car rolled to a stop near the pumps. As Dad rolled his window down, the man picked up the gas pump nozzle and asked, "Hi-test or regular?"

Augustus asked, "What's he doing, Dad?"

Dad laughed. "I guess they still pump the gas for you here, the way they used to a long time ago."

Phoebe smiled. "Cool! I bet you wish all gas stations did that!"

Dad smiled at the man. "Regular is fine, thank you, sir. I'm Truman Keen."

The man started filling the car, looking at Dad with curiosity. "Good to meet you, Truman. I'm Donny Gilmore. You need the oil or the wiper fluid checked?"

Dad shook his head. "I think we're in good shape. But thanks!"

"Just passing through?" Donny asked.

Dad smiled. "We're here for a little while to help a friend. And truth be told, we're really interested in researching the stories we've heard about the Black Opal's Curse. What can you tell me about it?"

Augustus and Phoebe leaned in so they didn't miss anything.

Donny nodded, his friendly expression suddenly turning serious. "Oh, yeah. It's real all right. When I was a kid, my grandparents farmed up in this area, and every well in a fifty-mile radius of the mine dried up within months of each other. Without water, of course, nothing would grow, not even the weeds, and they all blamed that Blackwood lady's curse."

Phoebe squinted up at the man and said, "If a community uses well water faster than the aquifers can be replenished by rainfall, the groundwater will be depleted and wells will dry up. Could that be what happened?"

Donny glanced at Phoebe with a confused expression, then continued on as if she hadn't said a word. "And back about thirty years ago, my cousin Roger was the star high school quarterback, and he had a terrible knee injury right at the beginning of the season. Ruined his knee so bad that he could never play football again, and my folks said it was that darned curse. And then a few years after that, the town built some new little league dugouts, and not a week later we had the biggest dust storm anybody's ever seen in these parts. Seventy mile-an-hour winds and a thousand-foot wall of desert sand, and those dugouts were completely destroyed."

Phoebe rolled her eyes. "Dust storms are just a form of wind erosion, and the dry desert climate means dust storms are bound to happen in this part of the country. What would a curse have to do with it?"

Donny put his hands on his hips. "All those bad things, one after the other? What else could it be?" He shook his head. "No, it's the curse all right. We never know when something bad is going to happen, but when it does, you can be sure that blasted curse is to blame."

Just then a slender dark-haired woman came out of the gas station with a water bottle. "Drink up, Donny!" she said with a smile. "It's hotter than jalapenos out here!" She nodded toward Dad and the kids and said, "Hi there. I'm Doreen, Donny's wife."

Donny guzzled some water, handed the bottle back to his wife, and finished pumping the gas. "Doreen, these nice folks were asking some questions about the curse," he said as he tightened the gas cap.

Doreen nodded. "We get people who stop in town from time to time and ask about it. Some people even take pictures of the mine where they say it all started. It's kinda crazy! Oh, Donny," she said. "Harriet Longfellow called and needs to bring her Cadillac in for a tire rotation later this week."

Augustus thought he saw a flicker of fear on Donny's face, but it was gone so quickly he thought he imagined it. Donny simply took a deep breath and nodded.

"We met Ms. Longfellow earlier today," Augustus said. "She was nice." He hoped what he said wasn't considered a lie. While she had seemed rude and condescending, she *had* given them lollipops, which was a nice gesture.

Doreen leaned against the gas pump with her arms crossed. "Hah! *Nice* isn't the first word that comes to mind," she said as she rolled her eyes. "I think she's a - -"

"Doreen!" Donny said harshly with a sharp shake of his head.

Doreen clamped her mouth closed, and then cleared her throat. "Anyway, Ms. Longfellow told me all about some guy trying to say he's found another big opal up in that mine, but it's a fake."

Dad glanced at each of the kids in surprise, and then appeared to choose his words carefully as he addressed Doreen. "Actually, I'm a certified gemologist, and can assure you it's the real deal. I've met the man who discovered it, and we took a look at the opal today. It's a beauty! Totally authentic."

Doreen looked at Donny with a frown. Then she shrugged and said, "Well, I guess sometimes Harriet has been known to … twist things."

"I'm sure everything will eventually come to light," Dad said with an easy smile. Reaching for his wallet he asked, "What do I owe you for the gas?"

"That'll be thirty-five even," Donny said. After giving Dad change for two twenties, he leaned against Dad's door and said, "I mind my business and such, but I gotta warn you about that curse. It's no joke."

Dad smiled. "I really appreciate the concern, but we believe that God is much more powerful than any curse, and that we don't have to be afraid."

Donny stepped back, his mouth open in shock. Doreen shook her head in disbelief and said, "Well, you seem like nice people, so you better watch yourselves, especially around the Longfellows. I'd hate to hear about anything bad happening."

Dad started up the car and said, "Thanks so much for the gas!"

Phoebe shook her head as they drove from the gas station back toward the KOA. "What is *with* all these people and the constant blaming every bad thing on a curse?" she asked.

Dad offered a sympathetic smile. "When people experience hardship, they sometimes feel like they need to find a reason for it, or they look for someone or something to blame," he explained.

"Do you think any of those things Mr. Gilmore mentioned could *actually* be caused by that hundred-year-old curse?" Augustus asked.

Dad shook his head. "I'm not one to look for a demon lurking behind every bush. Sometimes bad weather is just bad weather, and sometimes a knee injury is just that. Can demonic influence cause those things? Of course. Do people sometimes deal with the effects of curses that were spoken in the past? Sure they do. But I guess I'm withholding my assessment until we know more."

Augustus smiled. "I guess it's time for some mystery solving, Dad!"

Dad laughed and said, "Not before we get some groceries. The pantry is bare!"

Chapter 7 – A Bit of Misfortune

"Seems like it's impossible to just get the facts in this town!" Phoebe said as she rolled her eyes.

They had stopped for lunch at Milly's Diner before getting a week's worth of groceries at the local Piggly Wiggly. Phoebe and Augustus were helping Dad load the groceries from the cart into the trunk as Phoebe expressed her frustration. "I mean, it would be great to post your fuse box sabotage video to social media, Gus. Then people will know once and for all that the curse had nothing to do with the electricity going out. Even if we can't prove any of the other things that happened, we at least know for sure that someone cut those wires."

Augustus shook his head and said, "I think we need to wait. A stakeout at the visitor's center might help us figure out who cut those wires. And we might even need to keep an eye on the sheriff; see what he's up to, and what his deal is. I don't trust him."

Phoebe nodded. "And Ms. Longfellow too, while we're at it. There's something... I don't know. There's something about the way people react around her, or even the way they talk about her. It doesn't give me the warm fuzzies."

They all climbed into the car and dad cranked the engine and turned on the air. "We have to remember, though, that we aren't to judge the sheriff or Ms. Longfellow, or to wish any ill on either one of them," he admonished gently as he maneuvered the car out of the parking lot. "We represent Jesus everywhere we go, and even when it's obvious that someone is lying or hiding something, we can never take God's place as judge. Scripture is very clear about that."

Augustus sighed. "I know. But it's so hard sometimes!"

"No kidding!" Phoebe responded. "She just seemed so full of herself back there in the diner, like she was getting all puffed up when she talked about her family's reputation and how long they've lived here and all she's done and stuff."

Dad nodded. "Pride is a sneaky thing," he said. "Have you ever heard the Scripture that says pride goes before a fall?"

Augustus and Phoebe both nodded.

"What do you think it means, though, when it comes to Ms. Longfellow?" Augustus asked.

Dad shrugged. "Well, it seems like a warning that if we choose to partner with pride, I think it gives the enemy access to mess with us and to interfere in our lives. So I guess what I'm saying is that we should be praying for the sheriff and for Ms. Longfellow, for God to reveal himself to them and to bring truth and humility into their lives. Remember what you've been taught about the enemy?"

Phoebe sighed. "People are never the enemy," she quoted half-heartedly. "Our only enemy is satan."

Dad grinned and offered her a fist bump. "Exactly! And that includes the sheriff, Ms. Longfellow, and the whole town of Dead Nettle."

"So what did the electrician say?" Augustus asked. "Didn't you say Mr. Bragg was calling someone?"

Dad nodded as they turned into the KOA. "I got a text a little bit ago. Just so happens the only electrician in town already has a standing contract for emergency repair for any county building, so a team will be there first thing in the morning to fix it."

"Wouldn't the mayor or somebody important have to call to get that done?" Phoebe asked.

Dad shrugged. "I guess Mr. Bragg made enough noise about it that the mayor made it happen."

As the Mini-Cooper pulled up behind the Winnebago, Augustus noticed the camper listing to one side. "Uh, Dad?" he asked, pointing to two flat tires on the camper's right side.

"Bummer!" said Dad as he put the car in park. "Let's get these groceries unloaded first. Gus, I'd love your help to get the tires changed out afterward."

A short while later Phoebe was sitting in a camp chair in the shade watching Dad and Augustus take the flat tires off the Winnebago when a school bus pulled up to the campground entrance. Phoebe recognized Landon from the diner the day before. He made his way to their site. "What's up?" he asked.

"Flat tire," she said matter-of-factly. "Well, flat tires, plural. Two, to be exact."

Landon's brows went up. "What did I tell you? Looks like the curse is affecting you guys as well. I figured as much."

Phoebe threw her hands in the air. "It's not a curse when you drive over a nail," she insisted. "Front tire had a nail; back tire had a screw, so ... no curse involved."

Landon cocked his head sideways. "You know, back in the diner the other day your dad said you guys are into religion and stuff," he said.

Phoebe looked at him quizzically. "It's not religion," she said. "I mean, some people might call it that, but that's not how it is. Jesus is real, and he's alive, and we try to be like him and do the stuff he did."

Landon squinted at Phoebe. "My Grandma always lumped him in with Buddha and Vishnu and Zeus and all those guys. Are you saying he's different from all those other dudes?"

Phoebe smiled. "Absolutely!" she said with a firm nod.

Landon crossed his arms and said, "You can't see him though. Hard to believe in something you can't see."

"What about the wind?" Phoebe asked as she gestured to the air. "Can you see that?"

Landon looked around and said, "Well, not really, but you can see what the wind does. You can see the effects of the wind."

"Exactly!" Phoebe answered. "It's the same with Jesus. Maybe we can't physically see him, but we can see the things he does."

Landon seemed about to respond when Augustus bounded up to them. "Yo, Landon!" he said. "What's up?"

Landon gave Augustus a fist bump. "Nothing much; just got home from school."

Augustus looked at Phoebe. "Dad needs to take the tires into town to get fixed, so we're just gonna chill here for the rest of the afternoon."

"Wanna go swimming?" Landon offered. "The pool is open, and it's a thousand degrees out here!"

Phoebe jumped up from her chair with a grin. "It's one hundred and two degrees, to be exact, but the pool sounds awesome!"

Landon turned on his heel and ran, and yelled back over his shoulder. "Last one in the pool is a rotten egg!"

Chapter 8 – Danger in the Mine

Even though Augustus and Phoebe swam all afternoon, they barely slept a wink that night knowing they'd finally get to make a trip into the heart of the Blackwood Mine. To beat the heat of the day, they all rose at four-thirty the next morning, ate a quick breakfast of bagels and cream cheese, and donned sturdy hiking boots before heading into town in the Mini-Cooper. Mr. Bragg was waiting for them in his Jeep at the bed and breakfast, so they all climbed in just as the light began to show on the horizon.

"Mr. Bragg, I've got rope, binoculars, and walkie-talkies," Augustus announced as he patted his backpack.

Phoebe pointed to her backpack and added, "And I've got extra water bottles, first aid stuff, and my soil sample kit."

Mr. Bragg laughed. "You kids are prepared, that's for sure! And I brought safety helmets for all of us, the kind with built-in flashlights on the top. They're behind the back seat."

Dad smiled. "Gus, did you have a chance to do some more internet research about Miss Blackwood?"

Augustus nodded. "Only a little. But I actually found an article about her death from a 1972 newspaper. It mentioned she was a widow, and that she was an immigrant that had come to the U.S. in 1899 with her father and sister from an *unspecified European country*," Augustus explained, putting air quotes around the last three words. "Apparently her dad brought enough gold with him at the time to buy 1000 acres of land on the spot, and they lived in a tiny one-room cabin not far from the entrance to the mine. Want to see what she looked like?" he asked, holding up the phone.

Phoebe's eyes went wide as she stared at the grainy black and white photo on her brother's phone. The woman was tall and broad-shouldered, with a thick head of white hair that seemed to fly out from her head in every direction. She was dressed in pitch-black clothing, snarling at whoever was unlucky enough to be taking the photo. Even though the dark-eyed woman was far from the camera, the intense hatred in her gaze was crystal clear.

Dad took the phone and smiled sadly at the photo. "I know she looks pretty scary, and that people called her a witch," he said tenderly. "But remember that she's still a child of God, even if she chooses to partner with darkness."

Mr. Bragg looked quizzically at Dad. To Augustus it seemed as though the miner was about to ask Dad a question, but then decided against it.

Fifteen minutes later the Jeep bounced up a nearly invisible desert road, eventually coming to rest at the top of the arid outcropping that was home to the Billings Mine. Augustus hopped from the Jeep. Even though it was barely dusk, he did a 360-degree search of the terrain with his binoculars. "Looks clear!" he announced. "Only passable road is the one we just came up."

Mr. Bragg grabbed the helmets from behind the seat. As he passed them around, he said, "Safety rules: always wear your helmet, and *always* stick with a buddy. No one wanders off by themselves!"

Augustus put on the helmet, shouldered his backpack, and asked, "I've seen on the news about mines collapsing sometimes. Is this one dangerous?"

Mr. Bragg shook his head with a rueful smile. "If I thought it was dangerous, I wouldn't let you go inside! This mine is quite stable, and my crew and I have been in and out of these passages for the last two years without any problems." He pointed to a wood-and-rubble-strewn opening in the sandstone a few dozen yards to the right. "That was the original entrance to the mine," he explained. "This side collapsed in 1917, literally hours after the Billings Opal was extracted, but thankfully none of the miners were inside. After I bought the property, I studied the lay of the land with a drone and found the other entrance, which is pretty much a straight shot to the opposite side of this one."

"Cool!" Phoebe said as she donned her helmet. "Maybe we'll see some troglobites while we're in there!"

Augustus laughed and said, "What in the world is… whatever you just said?"

"Troglobite," she repeated. "It's an animal that lives entirely in the dark parts of caves. I've only seen them in nature videos."

"After you, Conrad!" Dad said.

They made their way around the base of the rocky outcropping, and in less than fifteen minutes they arrived at the entrance. A steel grated security door covered a man-sized hole in the rock that was slightly taller than Dad. When Augustus saw the opening he said, "I guess the gate makes sure nobody can just walk right in there and steal any opals."

Mr. Bragg laughed as he unlocked the gate, and the metal hinges emitted an ear-piercing squeal as he pulled it all the way open. "True! But the gate is more for safety than anything. I would hate for some hikers to wander down in here without flashlights or helmets and have some sort of accident, or get lost in the tunnels." He switched on his helmet lamp as he entered the mine. "Watch your step!"

Phoebe switched on her headlamp and went in behind Mr. Bragg, and Augustus followed suit with Dad bringing up the rear. "This is awesome!" Augustus yelled, enjoying the echo of his voice through the darkened passageways.

"Definitely a lot chillier in here than outside," Phoebe observed as she reached out to touch the smooth walls. "Were these tunnels formed with dynamite?"

Mr. Bragg continued walking forward. "Yep! The Billings family did most of the really hard work, blasting out passages to get to the opal veins."

Initially wide enough for just one person at a time, the tunnel widened out a few dozen yards into the mine as the passageway began to slope slightly downward. Augustus snapped photos with his phone as remnants of the century-old mining operation began to appear. "Cool! Check out these old metal rail tracks in the ground!"

Mr. Bragg called back over his shoulder. "These rails go all the way to the other side, to the collapsed entrance you saw from the Jeep. Oh, and speaking of dynamite, don't pick up or touch *anything* unless I can take a look at it first," he warned. "There's a chance you could see some hundred-year-old sticks of dynamite tucked into the nooks and crannies, or even stored in a box. I haven't seen any myself, but it's possible you'll see some, and it's *extremely* unstable, especially if it looks like crystals have formed on the outside where the old nitroglycerin has seeped out."

"Unstable dynamite?" Phoebe echoed with wide eyes. "Awesome!"

The air in the passageway became drier and stuffier, and wooden support beams began to appear across the tops and sides of the tunnel as they ventured farther in.

Suddenly a cloud of warm black air whooshed into the mine, filling the space above their heads with hundreds of tiny squeaking noises. Everyone ducked as Phoebe yelled, "*Bats*!"

The bats were unaccustomed to finding humans in their way on their daily return to roost at sunrise. They began to swarm around the heads of the grown-ups with ear-piercing squeaks.

Phoebe dropped to her hands and knees and pointed further down the passageway. "Let's go!" she yelled to her brother as Dad and Mr. Bragg covered their heads.

Shocked at how noisy the bats were, Augustus followed his sister and shimmied forward on hands and knees as dust began to be stirred up by the beating of many dozens of bats' wings.

"Look! There's a skinny little tunnel to the right up here!" Phoebe yelled just before she disappeared around the corner.

Augustus thought he heard Mr. Bragg yell something, but the bats were too loud. He squeezed into the narrow side tunnel behind Phoebe, and then sat on his haunches to catch his breath. That's when he noticed a skinny cardboard tube on a shallow ledge behind Phoebe's head.

He leaned over and peered closely at the tube, and when he read the faded writing on the label, his heart went cold.

"Feebs," he whispered, his heart pounding. "We need to back out very, very slowly, and watch where you put your hands and feet so you don't touch *anything*!"

Phoebe turned around and sucked in her breath when she saw what her brother was looking at. "It's a stick of dynamite!" she whispered. She looked down at the ground and saw another stick in the dust right next to her shoes. "And look! Both have those seeping nitroglycerin crystals Mr. Bragg warned us about.

Gus, these things could blow if we so much as breathe on them!"

Augustus backed slowly out of the tunnel on his hands and knees, no longer concerned about something as harmless as a swarm of bats. "Slow and steady, Feebs!" he urged.

He could tell she was holding her breath as she crawled slowly out of the tunnel. Back in the main passageway, they stopped and sat in the dirt, hearts pounding and limbs shaking. "Wow, that was close!" Phoebe managed with a shaky voice.

As they stood to their feet and dusted off their knees, neither one noticed the century-old shovel leaning against the wall. When they looked back on it later, neither Augustus nor Phoebe could remember touching the shovel, much less knocking it into the narrow tunnel from which they had just emerged.

The one with the unstable dynamite.

All they could remember was taking a few steps toward Dad, then freezing in terror as the sound of the falling shovel reached their ears.

They instinctively turned and ran deeper into the mine. Seconds later they were thrown to the ground by a deafening explosion, and everything went black.

Chapter 9 – Narrow Escape

"Feebs?" Augustus managed, his lips coated with dust and gritty sand. He wasn't sure how long he'd been lying in the rubble before he came to his senses. He felt around him on the ground, not sure where his backpack had gone.

He heard a little cough from somewhere close behind him. "I'm alive," she said weakly.

Augustus could barely hear his sister for the ringing in his ears, and he felt like he was talking underwater. "I'm coming!" he yelled.

He kicked his feet clear of some rubble and stood, grimacing at the sharp pain in his left ankle. He was grateful that nothing felt broken. The flashlight on his helmet was covered in a thick layer of dust, so he frantically dug through the rocks until he found what was left of his backpack. He breathed a sigh of relief when he found that the heavy-duty 900-lumen tactical flashlight inside was unscathed. "Where are you?" he yelled as he switched on the flashlight. "Can you stand?"

He saw Phoebe's arm shoot up from behind a pile of rubble a few feet away. "I'm okay," she said. He heard her spit a few times before she said, "Blech! There's dirt all in my mouth!"

Augustus knelt beside his sister and cleared the bigger pieces of rubble from her feet and legs as she rose to a sitting position, her backpack still on her shoulders and none the worse for wear. His relief that she wasn't seriously hurt bubbled up inside his chest, and he choked down a sudden sob. "I'm so glad you're okay!" he said, his voice shaky with emotion.

As she slowly stood and began trying to wipe some of the dust from her arms and legs, Augustus rose and went as close as he dared to the pile of stones blocking the mine shaft. "DAD!" he yelled as loudly as he could. "DAD!" he repeated. "MR. BRAGG! CAN YOU HEAR ME?!"

He held his breath and listened for a few long seconds, butterflies of fear beginning to creep into his belly as he his calls went unanswered.

Phoebe came to stand beside him, blinking as tears spilled from her eyes and her chin began to quiver. "I'm really scared, Gus," she managed. "I want Mom!"

Augustus nodded, digging deep down for courage. As he took a deep breath, boldness rose up in his chest with the instinct to protect his little sister. Taking her hand he calmly said, "I miss Mom too. We'll see her soon, and we can tell her all about our crazy adventures."

Phoebe's eyes went wide. "Do you think Dad's okay? And Mr. Bragg?"

Augustus swallowed hard and tried to imagine what Dad would do in this situation, and only one thing came to mind. "I think we should pray," he said with a firm nod, glad he sounded more confident than he felt.

Phoebe let out a ragged breath and nodded. "Okay," she managed with a little squeak as tears made patterns on her dusty cheeks.

Augustus remembered that Dad always said to pray to Jesus as if he was right there, so that's what he did. "Jesus, we need your help! The Bible says you are always with us, so I know you're with us right now in this mine. Thank you that we didn't get blown to smithereens, but we're really scared, and we don't know if Dad and Mr. Bragg are okay, and I really need to go to the bathroom!"

Phoebe nodded and said, "Me, too, Lord!"

Augustus continued, feeling no braver now than when he had started praying. "Anyway, we're asking for your help to get us out of here, God. Keep Dad and Mr. Bragg safe and help them find us. Amen."

Phoebe echoed, "Amen!"

Augustus stepped back and looked his sister up and down, afraid he might see blood everywhere. "Anything hurt?" he asked.

She groaned as stretched her arms over her head. "I don't think so, but I'm sure I'll be covered in a ton of bruises tomorrow, and there's dirt in places I didn't know dirt could be. You?"

He shrugged and said, "My mouth is full of sand, and my ankle isn't happy, but it's not so bad that I can't walk on it."

They looked toward the side of the tunnel where the explosion had happened and aimed their lights at the sides, top, and bottom. "Completely sealed up," Phoebe said matter-of-factly. She spun on her heel, pointing at the decades-old rail car tracks in the dirt beneath their feet. "I bet if we follow this, it'll lead us out to that old entrance." She grabbed her brother's hand and began pulling him forward as she started walking the only way they could go.

After ten minutes of following the mine car rails hand in hand, Augustus finally broke the silence. "Hey, Feebs. I need a break. Let's stop for a minute so I can rest my ankle." The ringing in his ears had mostly subsided, but his left ankle was now throbbing, and it felt tight and swollen inside his shoe.

They sat on the ground and pulled water bottles from their backpacks. After drinking a little, they each polished off a granola bar. "Too bad we don't have any ice," Augustus said as he tenderly rubbed his throbbing ankle.

Phoebe sat upright. "Oh my gosh! The first aid kit!" She rummaged through her dusty pack and pulled out a red zippered case. "There's one of those cold compress things that you crush and shake up in here. I totally forgot! Stick your leg out."

She found the cold pack, squeezed it to activate the ice crystals, and pressed it onto her brother's swollen ankle. Then she dug out an Ace bandage and carefully wrapped it around, securing the ice pack in place with the Velcro ends.

Augustus smiled through gritted teeth. "Ouch! And thanks!" he said.

48

He aimed the beam of the tactical flashlight toward the ceiling. "It's definitely wider and taller in this part of the tunnel," he said. Then something on the opposite wall caught his eye. "Wait, what is that?"

Phoebe looked to where the flashlight beam was pointing. "Is that some sort of writing?"

They both stood to get a closer look at the crudely formed lettering, and Augustus took out his phone and started snapping pictures. "I don't know what it says, but it gives me the heebie-jeebies, that's for sure."

"I'll get a video, too" Phoebe offered as she raised her phone and started filming. "It's definitely Latin. But number one, it's backwards, and number two, I don't read Latin." She leaned in closely and wrinkled her nose. "And what kind of paint is this?" she asked.

Augustus felt the hairs stand up on the back of his neck as he examined the dark brownish-red pigment. "It's heebie-jeebie paint," he said.

Just then his foot kicked something on the ground, and he glanced down to see what it was. A small wooden bowl lay in the dirt, stained with the same dark pigment that was on the wall. As he snapped photos of it he said, "Oh, look, a heebie-jeebie bowl for the heebie-jeebie paint!"

At that moment a faint sound reached their ears.

"Did you hear that?" Phoebe whispered.

"Be still, and turn off your head lamp!" Augustus urged.

They both extinguished their head lamps and remained motionless. When Augustus turned off his tactical flashlight, they were shocked to realize they

49

could see the smallest hint of light coming from far down the tunnel.

They heard the sound again, the unmistakable voice of Dad desperately calling their names. "*Augustus*! *Phoebe*!"

Augustus cupped his hands around his mouth and shouted as loudly as he could. "Dad! We're here! We're okay!" A sob caught in his throat as he whispered, "Thank you, Jesus!"

Phoebe switched her headlamp back on and started jogging toward the light.

"Feebs!" Augustus yelled. "Wait! We have to stay together, and I can't run!"

She stopped and waited for him to catch up and said, "If I could run and carry you piggyback, I would, but that's not happening!"

Augustus laughed and took her hand. "Well, it's the thought that counts!"

As they made their way toward their Dad's voice, Augustus was suddenly choked up with gratitude as he whispered a prayer.

Thank you, Jesus!

Chapter 10 – The Writing on the Wall

Mr. Bragg sat at the tiny RV dinner table with his head in his hands.

"You couldn't have known, Conrad," Dad said gently.

Augustus nodded as he polished off a large bowl of macaroni and cheese. "It was just a freaky accident," he said. "We should have stayed with you and ignored those bats."

Mr. Bragg shook his head. "I've walked by that side tunnel countless times, and it only extends about half a dozen feet, so I never explored it." He looked up at Dad with tear-filled eyes and said, "I'm paying every penny of their emergency room bill, and I'm not taking no for an answer!"

Dad clapped Mr. Bragg on the shoulder and nodded. "It's not necessary, but thank you."

Augustus sat with his leg elevated, a pair of crutches leaning against the back of his chair. "Dad, we saw something inside the mine you really need to see," he said as he pulled out his phone.

Dad pulled the phone closer and began scrolling through the photos of the writing they had discovered.

"That's bizarre," he said quietly, zooming in on the photos. "It's in Latin, but it's written backwards."

Phoebe emerged just then with her hair wrapped in a towel. "Hope all that dirt doesn't clog up the shower drain, Dad!"

Mr. Bragg looked at her, his brows furrowed with concern. "How are you feeling?"

Phoebe gave him two thumbs up. "Good as new!" she said. "I'm a little sore all over, and tomorrow I imagine my bruises will have bruises. But that shower hit the spot."

She sat down and looked at Dad, wide-eyed. "I'm sorry I crawled off ahead, Dad," she said quietly. Looking at the floor with a trembling chin she added, "I could have killed us all and it would have been my fault."

Dad wrapped her in a bear hug. "Feebs, no, sweetie! It was an accident!" He kissed her forehead and hugged her again. "God was with all of us in that mine, that's for sure, and don't you dare believe the lie that it was your fault, okay?"

Phoebe nodded and offered him a teary smile. "Okay," she managed.

"My turn for the shower!" Augustus said. "Feebs, where's your phone? I'm showing them what we found on the wall in there."

Phoebe dug her phone from her backpack and played the video. "It was really weird," she said as Dad and Mr. Bragg leaned in to watch it.

"Can you make out what's written there?" Mr. Bragg asked.

Dad stood abruptly and moved toward the front of the RV. He held Augustus's phone up to the rear view mirror, and as he read the text in the photo, his eyes went wide as saucers. Then he came back to the table and sat down slowly, his expression serious.

"What is it, Dad?" Augustus asked. "Can you read it?"

Dad nodded. "I can," he said quietly.

Phoebe set her water bottle down and asked, "Well? What's it say?"

Dad took a deep breath and said, "I will not repeat what it says." He looked at Mr. Bragg, and then at each of his children. "It's a curse on the town of Dead Nettle."

Mr. Bragg waved him off. "Oh, Truman, be serious."

Dad looked at him sharply. "This is not something I'd make a joke about, Conrad," he said. "It's a curse that invokes sickness, death, and pestilence on the town, written backwards in what I can only assume is blood."

Augustus swallowed hard and pointed at Phoebe. "Told you!" he said. "Heebie-jeebie bowl with heebie-jeebie paint!" To Dad he said, "I guess the rumors about Merletta Blackwood being a witch must be true then."

Dad looked at each of them in turn. "But we know that God is more powerful than any curse, and a single believer is more powerful than a room full of witches," he said with a firm nod.

Mr. Bragg clearly wasn't buying it. "I don't believe in demons or witches or ghosts or the bogeyman, or any of that bunkum," he said with a shrug. "I believe there is a god out in the universe, I guess, like a Supreme Maker or whatever. But all those other things are just silly campfire stories people tell to keep their kids in line."

Augustus shook his head. "Dude! If you had seen half the stuff we've seen, you'd know that demons and witches are real. Hundred percent."

Dad nodded and said, "And we have absolutely *nothing* to fear from them, because Christ is in us, and He who is in us is greater than he who is in the world."

Mr. Bragg threw up his hands. "What does that even mean?" he asked.

"The Bible tells us we have authority," Dad explained gently. "We follow Jesus, and that means that the power that raised Jesus from the dead is alive inside each of us. Jesus gave his followers – that means us – power and the authority to heal the sick, cast out demons, and overcome evil in the world. We've seen it, time and time again."

Mr. Bragg crossed his arms, his brow furrowed. "Explain. What have you seen?"

Dad smiled. "I know you've heard the one story of our demonic encounter with that man at the Miami convention. You said yourself it's one of the reasons you asked me to come here."

Mr. Bragg nodded. "What else? That's just one incident."

Augustus said, "We were in Kenya last year, and the local witch doctor didn't want us to be there, and he did all sorts of magic ritual stuff to try and hex us or scare us into leaving."

Phoebe wrinkled her nose. "It was gross! Those poor chickens!"

"But we prayed," Dad said. "We gathered with a handful of Christians who lived in the village. We invited the Holy Spirit to come and we rebuked the demons, and when we did that, the witch doctor screamed and ran out of the village. It's been a year, and my friends there tell me he has never come back."

"Mr. Bragg, I found it really hard to believe at first, too," Phoebe added. "I guess you could say I'm a natural-born doubter. But we've seen too much for me to be able to explain it away. There was this one time in Haiti when we had a run-in with an angry voodoo priestess, and she was … let's just say '*unpleasant.*'"

"You mean to tell me voodoo is actually real?" Mr. Bragg asked. "I thought it was just in the movies! Or at the very least, just some kind of earth-worship religion or something."

"Oh, it's very real," Dad explained. "It's a blend of West African beliefs mixed with the worship of Catholic saints, all stirred together with a big splash of black magic and sorcery."

"How do you know they aren't just worshipping the same God you do, just in a different way that looks strange to you because of their culture?" Mr. Bragg asked.

Dad smiled. "We believe the Bible is the word of God, for starters. That's what we follow, the *only* book we follow, and it tells us there is one true God and that we cannot worship any other god. It also tells us, quite clearly, that we are never to consult with witches or take part in sorcery. What we saw in that Haitian village was a deceived, angry, bitter woman that sought to control people by inflicting sickness, accidents, and even death." He shook his head in wonder and added, "The priestess was intimidating and powerful, for sure. And she had a great deal of influence in her community. It took a week of prayer and fasting, but seven days after we started praying, the priestess had a supernatural encounter with the Holy Spirit. She submitted to Jesus, repented of all of her sorcery, and ended up leading just about the whole village to Christ. It was something else!"

Phoebe said, "You know, Mr. Bragg, I was wondering why you haven't seen that creepy writing on the wall before now."

Mr. Bragg nodded. "The part of the mine where you saw this is exactly where the first opal was mined in 1917, and now it's considered too unstable," he explained. "We found a rich opal vein in a tunnel that ran perpendicular to the main passage, so my crew and I never wanted or needed to go down the tunnel where you saw this."

"That makes sense," Augustus said.

Mr. Bragg stared out the window, lost in thought for a moment. Then he looked at Augustus and Phoebe in turn and said, "I'm just glad neither of you was seriously injured today."

"Dad, what do we do about the curse?" Augustus asked. "We can't just pretend it isn't there."

Dad smiled and said, "We'll do what we always do in these situations. We pray." He glanced up at Mr. Bragg and said, "We'd love for you to join us, Conrad."

Mr. Bragg rose from the seat and said, "Thanks, but I think I'll leave that to you. I'm going back to the B&B." He extended his hand to Dad and as he shook it he added, "You've given me a LOT to think about, Truman."

Chapter 11 – Threats

Augustus and Phoebe were grateful that Dad declared Thursday a day of ice packs, rest, and recuperation. Their bodies were stiff and sore from their brush with a cave-in, and throughout the day they each took time to thank God their injuries weren't severe.

Just before lunch on Friday, Dad and the kids drove back into town to meet Mr. Bragg at the visitor's center. As they pulled into a parking spot, they found themselves next to a tricked out red pickup truck taking up two handicapped spots directly in front of the main entrance. The truck had massive off-road tires and shiny dual exhaust pipes. The body was lifted so high off the suspension that the average person would need a step stool to climb inside. As they walked around it, Augustus noticed a silver skull welded to the front of the truck as a hood ornament.

Augustus rolled his eyes and said, "That is one *ugly* truck!"

Phoebe snickered and said, "Can you imagine how much gas that thing drinks?"

Dad opened the visitor's center door so Augustus could make it through on his crutches first, and they found themselves face to face with two muscular college-aged men wearing black t-shirts with the word SECURITY across the front. The men were clearly brothers, both with jet black crew cuts and similar deep-set brown eyes and dimples in their chins. They stood with their arms crossed, frowning as Dad and Phoebe entered.

"Morning!" Dad said jovially. Then he simply stepped around the two burly men and kept walking toward the utility closet in the breakroom.

Phoebe stepped up to the men and copied Dad. "Morning!" she said, then ducked around them.

Augustus nodded at them both, trying not to laugh at their dumbfounded expressions. "Hi!"

"You can't go in there!" one of them said as he whirled around and hurried toward the breakroom with his brother on his heels. "Our family owns this building, and we say where you can and can't go, Mister!"

Augustus wasn't surprised when Dad didn't stop walking. "I'm fairly certain this is a county-owned building," Dad said over his shoulder. "I'm checking on the electrician's repair progress." He stopped and turned around with his hand out. "Truman Keen," he announced with a broad smile. "And you are?"

The two men looked at each other, confused for a moment. Then each one shook Dad's hand briefly. To Augustus it seemed forced, as if their mom had made them do it. "Jacob Longfellow," said the first one. "This is my brother Campbell."

Campbell, slightly shorter than Jacob, glared up at his brother. "How many times I gotta tell you I can speak for myself?" he said under his breath.

Dad offered them both a genuine smile and said, "Good to meet you, gentlemen. These are my children, Phoebe and Augustus Blue."

Phoebe squinted up at the brothers. "Longfellow?" she asked. "Like Sheriff Longfellow, and Harriet Longfellow?"

The brothers nodded and crossed their arms again, suddenly smug. "Yep," Campbell said. "The sheriff's our uncle; Harriet Longfellow is our mom. And she's donated a ton of money to help get this center built, along with most of the stuff in here, so you might say our family *does* own it."

Dad nodded and said, "I see how that can make it seem like your family owns it, but I'm sure the county tax records would show differently. Oh!" Dad's eyes lit up. "I get it! You're volunteering to be security for the upcoming exhibition!"

Jacob and Campbell looked at each other blankly.

"My colleague Mr. Bragg is having an exhibition here to display the record-breaking opal he's found up at the Blackwood Mine," Dad explained. "The two of you acting as security guards is a fantastic idea!"

Jacob shook his head in frustration. "No, no, *no*! Our mom told us about this guy's opal being a big, fat fake, and the exhibit's not happening." He leaned forward and poked Dad in the chest with his stubby forefinger. "We're here to make *sure* of that." He snickered and elbowed his brother. "It's just a terrible shame it has to be cancelled, what with the curse and all."

Augustus looked back and forth between Dad and the self-appointed security guards, unsure how Dad would respond to Jacob's bullying.

The front door opened just then, and Mr. Bragg walked in followed by Sheriff Longfellow. Dad's face brightened and he stepped around Jacob and Campbell. "Ah! Good morning Conrad! I was just talking with these two strapping young men about being a security team for your exhibit."

Augustus watched as Campbell made a beeline for Sheriff Longfellow. "Ricky, don't Mama own this building?" he asked.

Sheriff Longfellow rolled his eyes. "No, you nitwit. This is a county building. Why?"

Campbell looked at the floor with a embarrassed huff. "Never mind."

Dad shook hands with the sheriff and Mr. Bragg. "Looks like we're all set to move forward with that exhibition, Conrad," he said. "Let's check out the new electrical breaker box."

To Augustus it sounded as if Campbell was actually whining. "But Ricky, you told us there's no way it's happening!"

The sheriff shook his head at Campbell, his lips pressed into a thin line. "Quiet," he growled softly.

Augustus made his way to a nearby chair where Phoebe was covertly recording the whole interaction on her phone. "Good thinking!" he whispered with a thumbs up.

She shrugged and whispered, "Both of those bouncers are focused on Dad, so I figured they wouldn't notice. Dad's just so... *calm*! I would've punched that dude in the face if he'd poked me like that!"

Augustus pulled up another chair and sat next to her. "Did you see how the sheriff reacted just now?"

Phoebe nodded. "Yep, and it's clear as day on the recording."

While Dad and Conrad checked out the revamped electrical work, the sheriff and his two cousins stood near the door, brooding silently. A few minutes later Dad and Mr. Bragg made their way toward the exit. "Hey kids, we're all done!" Dad called.

Phoebe kept recording as she and Augustus stood to follow Dad.

Jacob and Campbell stood with their arms crossed, blocking the front door. "You know, Mr. Keen, that curse ain't to be fooled with," Jacob said, staring hard at Dad.

Campbell nodded. "That's the truth! It can get downright *dangerous* around here if you're not careful."

Dad nodded and said, "Oh, I'm familiar with the stories, all right. But when it comes to the exhibition, I'm convinced it's somebody blowing a bunch of smoke." He shrugged and added, "And we believe God is bigger and more powerful than any curse, so we're not worried. But I appreciate your concern."

Jacob shrugged. "It's your funeral, buddy," he said.

"Yeah," Campbell echoed. "It's your funeral."

Sheriff Longfellow snapped his fingers and shouted, "Enough! Now you boys bid these folks a nice day and get on home to your mother!"

It was all Augustus could do not to laugh out loud at the humbled expressions on the Longfellow brothers' faces as they stomped out the door toward the pickup truck. As they climbed into the cab the sheriff leaned his head out of the visitor's center door and yelled, "And if you boys park in that handicapped spot one more time, you'll find that truck in the impound lot!"

The sheriff held the door open so Augustus and his crutches could go out first. "My apologies, Mr. Keen," the sheriff said with a broad smile that didn't reach his eyes. "Sometimes those boys don't have a lick of sense in their heads."

Dad waved him off with a smile. "No harm done," he said kindly. To Augustus and Phoebe he asked, "Milly's for lunch?"

"Sounds good!" Augustus said as he tossed his crutches in the back seat and climbed in.

As they drove out of the parking lot, Augustus watched in the rear view mirror as the sheriff's fake smile faded into an angry scowl.

Chapter 12 – Explosion!

After a filling breakfast of pancakes and sausage in the RV, the family headed back into Dead Nettle just before ten on Saturday morning. "So why are we going back again today?" Augustus asked. "I thought you already checked the electrical system and it's good to go."

Dad nodded and said, "Yep, the electricity is fine. Mr. Bragg wants to go over the exhibit layout and come up with something new. He wants to rearrange the displays in a more interesting setup than how it looks now; more like an art gallery and less like a visitor's center."

"Makes sense!" said Phoebe.

As they approached Dead Nettle, Augustus pointed up the street ahead. "Hey! There's the Longfellow brothers in that ugly red truck again!" he said.

They all watched the big truck peel out of the visitor's center parking lot and race out of town in the opposite direction.

"I don't trust them," Phoebe said with a furrowed brow.

"Neither do I!" said Augustus.

"Guys, let's give them the benefit of the doubt," Dad said gently as they drove in and parked next to Mr. Bragg's Jeep. "Maybe they were just having breakfast at Milly's across the street. It looks like her parking lot is almost full, and it's too small for that over-sized truck."

Augustus looked at Phoebe and shook his head. "Maybe," said he said, unconvinced. He leaned forward and whispered to his sister. "I wouldn't be surprised if they were up to something!"

Dad turned off the car and hopped out. "Right on time!"

"The center should be open normal hours now, right?" Phoebe asked as she and Augustus climbed out of the car. "The sign shows 10:00 to 3:00 Monday through Saturday, and Noon to 4:00 on Sunday."

"Yep," he answered. They went inside and were surprised to see Brenda Conner behind the welcome desk on the right just inside the door.

"Well, hello, again!" said Brenda. "Mr. Bragg is washing up in the restroo - - -"

*Ka-**BOOM**!!!!!!*

Her voice was cut off by an explosion coming from the direction of the bathrooms located behind the welcome desk. Water began trickling under the door toward Brenda's feet almost immediately.

Dad rushed into the restroom. "Conrad!" he called frantically. "Are you okay?"

Augustus hobbled closer so he could see through the open door. Two miniature geysers were spewing water from what used to be two toilet tanks. The seats

65

and bowls were mostly intact, lying sideways on the rapidly flooding floor, but the toilet tanks were nearly obliterated.

Mr. Bragg slowly walked from the room, dripping from head to toe and bleeding profusely from a cut above his left eye. "I think I'll live," he said quietly.

"Feebs! First aid kit!" Dad called. "I'll get paper towels!"

"On it!" Phoebe yelled. She raced to the car and was back inside in a flash with the red zippered case and an empty water bottle.

"Oh dear, oh dear, oh dear!" wailed Brenda as she wrung her hands, slowly backing away from the encroaching water.

Phoebe pulled Brenda's rolling chair to the middle of the room and guided Mr. Bragg to it. "We need to clean that cut first thing," she said firmly. "You may need stitches."

Mr. Bragg nodded and dutifully sat down as he took several deep breaths. Dad brought a fat roll of paper towels from the breakroom.

As Phoebe gently cleaned the cut, Mr. Bragg said, "I have no clue what just happened. I didn't even use the toilet! I was washing my hands one minute, and the next, the toilets exploded; both of them at the *exact* same time! The bathroom is full of a thousand shards of ceramic, so if you go in there, Truman, watch your step!"

At that moment, the front door opened and Sheriff Longfellow strode in.

"Well, that was conveniently fast," Augustus whispered to Dad.

"Everybody out!" the sheriff demanded. "This building is condemned!"

Brenda scurried to her car with a fearful backward glance at the water that had begun to flow across the linoleum and out the front door.

Phoebe barely acknowledged the interruption. "Don't get up yet, Mr. Bragg," she said. "I've almost got this butterfly bandage all set."

Dad and Augustus lounged against the welcome desk, making no move to exit even as water began to flow beside their shoes.

"Can't you people hear?" the sheriff asked. "I said this building is condemned, and you all need to leave *now*!"

Dad crossed his arms and said, "Why in the world would the building be condemned, Sheriff?" he asked.

The Sheriff pointed to the water gushing from the bathrooms. "Are you blind?" he asked, his voice getting louder with every word. "Raw sewage!"

Phoebe laughed out loud. "The water that fills a toilet tank is not raw sewage," she said calmly. "This is just city water coming from the main pipes, the exact same water that we drink from the water fountain. Besides, if it was raw sewage, we'd all smell it."

"Where's the main water shut-off valve?" Dad asked amiably. "I'm happy to go shut it off for you."

"Everybody out this *instant*!" the sheriff shouted, his face turning red with anger. He stomped through the flowing water toward the welcome desk and

67

grabbed a tape dispenser. Then he pulled a yellow piece of paper from his back pocket and splashed to the front door. He wasted no time taping the paper to the glass as he said, "It's officially condemned by the city, and if you don't leave immediately, I will arrest every one of you for criminal trespass! Now *move*!"

Dad came to stand next to Mr. Bragg. "How are you feeling?" he asked. "Are you dizzy or light-headed or anything?"

Mr. Bragg gave two thumbs up as he rose from the chair, still soaking wet. "All good! May need some aspirin, but thanks to that daughter of yours, I'm not gushing blood any longer," he said, heading toward the door. He stopped on his way out and stared hard at the sheriff. "I don't know what game you're playing, Sheriff," he said quietly. "But we're onto you, and we'll get to the bottom of this, you can be sure."

The sheriff narrowed his eyes at Mr. Bragg. "Well, now, that sounds an awful lot like a threat to me, mister," he said, his voice nearly a growl.

Mr. Bragg shrugged. Just before he stepped outside he said, "Consider it a promise."

Augustus was inspired by Mr. Bragg's bravery. As he made his way outside, he said loudly, "Well, Dad, I have absolutely *no* idea how Sheriff Longfellow miraculously knew about the toilets exploding just seconds after it happened, but *gosh*, we sure are lucky!"

Augustus could see Phoebe covering her mouth, trying not to laugh.

The Sheriff was focused on holding the door open as Augustus maneuvered through with his crutches.

Phoebe ducked behind the welcome desk and went down on all fours, splashing the whole way. "Now where is my water bottle?" she asked loudly.

"*Out!*" screamed the sheriff.

Phoebe popped up from behind the desk with her water bottle a moment later. "Found it!" she said.

Once they were all inside the car, the three of them looked at each other, bewildered. "What just happened?" Augustus asked with an incredulous shake of his head.

Phoebe held up her bottle, both arms dripping wet. "I got a water sample, and we can test it for contaminants back at the RV," she said. "I'll bet you ten bucks this water is clean enough to drink, and I'll bet you another ten that Sheriff Longfellow's nephews had something to do with this."

Dad started the car, lost in thought for a moment.

Then he looked up toward the sky and said, "Jesus, thank you that Conrad wasn't badly hurt today! I ask for quick healing for his body, and for a hedge of protection around him. Lord, we have no idea what's going on here, and we need your wisdom! Will you uncover everything that's hidden, and bring the truth to light? Trip up the plans of the enemy in this town, and guide us. Amen."

Augustus and Phoebe echoed. "Amen!"

Chapter 13 – Another Close Call

With Augustus still nursing his sprained ankle, they decided to postpone their family hike. They crowded around the RV dining table after lunch and called Mom on video chat.

"Now remember," Dad said. "We don't want to worry Granny, and I've been keeping Mom filled in with texts, so if Granny gets on the call, there's no need to mention all the mine collapsing and toilets exploding. Deal?"

Augustus and Phoebe nodded.

Although they were calling Mom's phone, Granny Shaefer's sweet, wrinkled face filled the screen as she answered. "Granny!" Augustus and Phoebe said in unison.

"Well, look who it is!" Granny said. "How are my two adventurous grandchildren today?"

"We're good," Augustus said. He glanced over his shoulder, relieved that his crutches weren't in view on the camera. Then he gestured to the swimsuit he was wearing and said, "We're going swimming in a little bit. It's *hot*!"

Granny shook her head and said, "Not quite warm enough here in North Carolina for outside swimming!" she said. "Maybe next month."

"Granny, how is your new hip?" Phoebe asked. "How's therapy?"

Granny Shaefer rolled her eyes. "I'm ready to stop being fussed over!" she said. "The doc says I'll be good as new before long. I can't wait to see you both!" She pulled the phone down and called, "Candace! The kids are on video chat!"

Granny blew a kiss and said, "Love you both; here's your mother."

"Hey, guys!" Mom said as her face came into view. "How's ... everything?" she said with a rueful smile.

"Good!" Augustus said. "We met one of the local kids, Landon, so we're going swimming with him in a bit."

"Mom! I'm doing a water sample to test for contamination," Phoebe said with a huge grin. "Trying to disprove someone's claim that there's raw sewage in the visitor's center."

"That sounds cool!" said Mom. "Dad said in his text that you were going to visit the local church tomorrow morning."

Augustus nodded. "Yep. I'm asking Landon if he wants to go with us."

"Great idea!" said Mom. "I've been praying for all three of you so much! Dad's been keeping me in the loop with ... stuff." She emphasized the last word with a little wink.

Knowing that Granny could likely hear the conversation, Augustus chose his words carefully. "This is a very... *interesting* place," he said. "Lots of people with some pretty weird ideas."

"And it's also really hot!" added Phoebe with a laugh. "I'm so glad there's a pool!"

"How much longer for Granny's therapy?" Augustus asked.

Mom smiled as she looked at Granny. "Four more weeks of hard work, I think, and she should be good as new. I can get out of Granny's hair and she can get back to her weekly bingo game."

"*GUS!*"

Dad's voice reverberated from the back of the RV, loudly and urgent.

"*Bring the shotgun!*"

Augustus glanced at Phoebe, wide-eyed. Then he smiled brightly at Mom and quickly said, "Um, well, ok, so we're gonna go help Dad! Miss you! Bye, Granny!"

Phoebe blew a kiss and said, "Love you both! We'll call tomorrow after church!"

Augustus could tell Mom was suddenly worried, so he leaned in close to the camera. "We're all good, Mom; promise. Love you!" Then he pushed the button to end the call.

"*GUS!*" Dad called.

"Coming!" he yelled toward Dad.

"What's wrong?" Phoebe asked, her brows furrowed.

"No clue," said Augustus as he grabbed his crutches and stood. "Dad's shotgun is under this bench we're sitting on, so hop up."

She jumped to her feet and lifted the seat cushion. The space underneath was filled with various supplies, and the shotgun was on top next to a box of ammunition.

Augustus loaded it quickly and handed it to Phoebe. "Hurry!" he said. "I can't carry it with these crutches."

Phoebe nodded and took the shotgun, careful to hold it safely as Dad had taught her as she rushed toward the back of the RV.

"Dad?" Augustus called.

Dad's voice came from inside the bedroom. "In here! Move *very* slowly!"

Phoebe inched open the sliding pocket door to the tiny bedroom. Dad stood stock still at the foot of the double bed without a shirt on, holding his hand out behind him. "Slowly," he said again.

Augustus came around the right as Phoebe carefully passed the shotgun to Dad.

"Back up," Dad said softly. "And plug your ears."

"What …?"

The question died in Augustus's mouth as his eyes landed on an enormous snake curled up on Dad's bed between the pillows. The room was filled with the eerie whir of the snake's rattling tail.

Phoebe sucked in a breath. "That's a Mohave rattler!" she said. She took a few small steps backward and added, "Dad, be careful! They're legit deadly!"

Dad's movements were slow and fluid as he raised the shotgun to his shoulder. "I know," he whispered. "Firing in three, two, one."

The kids both plugged their ears as Dad pulled the trigger, his aim true and lethal.

Augustus watched in fascination as the messy but headless snake writhed harmlessly on the bed. "That's so gross!" he said.

Dad let out the breath he had been holding and sank to the bed with his eyes closed. "Thank you, Jesus!" he whispered.

Phoebe ran from the room, returning a moment later carrying bright yellow rubber gloves and two trash bags. With a rueful smile she said, "One for the snake; the other for the blankets and pillow cases, to wash off all the snaky bits."

"How did that thing get in here?" Augustus asked.

Dad shrugged. "No clue," he said. "After all that's been happening, I really think we're under a spiritual attack." He grabbed a shirt from the nearby dresser and pulled it on over his head. "How about we step outside and do a prayer walk around the RV?" He glanced at the remains of the snake and laughed. "I'll clean this up afterward."

Phoebe left the gloves and trash bags on the bed, and the three of them made their way outside into the oppressive heat of the afternoon. Just as Phoebe closed the door behind her, Landon approached from the pool wearing his swim trunks.

"Hey, guys!" Landon said. "What's up?"

Dad smiled at Landon. "We're going to pray really quick if you want to join, and then I'm sure these guys would want to come swimming."

Landon cocked his head sideways and shrugged. "I don't really know how to pray and stuff, so I'll just watch, I guess." He leaned against a nearby tree and crossed his arms, his expression a mixture of curiosity and doubt.

Dad looked up at the sky and began to walk slowly around the RV with Phoebe and Augustus behind him. "Lord, we are so thankful for your love and protection," Dad prayed. "Your Word says we are priests and kings in your kingdom, and with the authority given to me by the risen Christ, I bind every demonic attack coming against us in Jesus name. I cast it into the pit, and I loose the peace and power of Jesus over all of us."

At that moment, a fresh-smelling wind began to blow and swirl around the RV. Landon looked around, startled, then fell into step close behind Augustus as they circled the campsite.

Dad continued. "Lord, dispatch your holy righteous angels to stand guard around this RV and around each one of us. I forbid anything from the kingdom of darkness to enter this RV and this campsite, and we decree that this space is safe and holy and consecrated to Yahweh. Jesus, we ask you to trip up the snares of the enemy, and to give us your wisdom and discernment. We acknowledge that you are more powerful than any curse, and I command fear and worry to disappear now as faith rises up in each of us. In Jesus' name, amen!"

Phoebe and Augustus echoed, "Amen!" as they came full circle around the RV.

Landon shook his head and said, "Man, that was really spooky. Did you feel that wind?"

Dad smiled. "The presence of God sometimes comes like a wind," he explained.

Landon nodded as he looked at Phoebe and said, "Huh. Like a wind."

"Hey, we want to visit the New Life Community Church in town tomorrow morning," Augustus said. "Wanna come with us? We saw it up the street from your grandma's diner."

Landon cocked his head sideways. "Church?" he asked. "Well, first thing, church isn't really my thing. And second, there's none left in Dead Nettle. The one church building you saw closed a few years ago. They keep the parking lot clean and keep the weeds trimmed and stuff, but I can't remember when I last saw people there. Anyway, you ready to swim?"

"You guys go ahead," Phoebe said. "I'll help Dad clean up the mess inside, and then I'll get my swimsuit on."

Dad gave Phoebe a sideways hug and said, "You know, after we get done in here, I think I could use a nice, relaxing swim myself!"

As Augustus followed Landon toward the pool, he glanced back over his shoulder, praying silently.

God, I know the Bible says not to fear, and that you've commanded us to be strong and courageous and all that, but that snake was too close for comfort! Vandalism, cave-ins, bullies, exploding toilets, and now a snake! What else does Dead Nettle want to throw at us?

Chapter 14 – Methods of Mischief

"We all know that toilets don't just explode by themselves," Phoebe said quietly as she sat down at one of several desks at the public library in Sandy Rock, an hour's drive from Dead Nettle. She plugged in her phone and laptop to charge and said, "Let's see what the internet can tell us about that!"

Dad nodded as he took a seat beside Phoebe, then plugged in his phone and laptop as well. "That electrical storm yesterday was intense!" he said, keeping his voice low. "You don't see lightning like that very often."

Augustus sat at a desk adjacent to Phoebe's. "I wonder how long it'll take a small town like Dead Nettle to replace the transformer at the KOA?" he asked.

Dad shrugged. "I'm guessing it could be at least a full day, maybe even longer," he said. "Gus, do you have an outlet under your desk where you can charge up, too?"

Augustus opened his laptop and gave Dad a thumbs up. "Yep; already plugged in. My phone and laptop were dead as doornails!"

With no power in the RV to charge their phones and laptops from late Sunday afternoon through Monday morning, they agreed they didn't want to waste all of their generator fuel to power the RV. They headed to the nearest town with a public library where they could spend a few hours doing homework, conducting research, and recharging all of their devices. The Sandy Rock Library did not disappoint, with plenty of desks with standard plugs and USB charging outlets.

After a few moments Dad said, "Oh, wow. It's an email from Harriet Longfellow, and she sounds a little miffed."

Augustus and Phoebe both stood, coming to flank Dad so they could lean in and read the email.

Dear Mr. Keen,

I trust this email finds you well, and I won't waste your time with further pleasantries. Due to the increased troubles of late, I must insist that you and your family wrap up your business in Dead Nettle and go back home as quickly as possible. I tried to warn you about the Black Opal's Curse, but you just didn't listen, and now we've got a sewage-filled visitor's center and campground with no power until who knows when.

79

The curse is real, Mr. Keen. The Blackwood Witch isn't just some myth. She is as real as you or me, and she is not to be trifled with. It would be best for all of us – your safety and ours – if you and Mr. Bragg would leave Dead Nettle well enough alone.

Yours sincerely,

Harriet Longfellow
Historian, Town of Dead Nettle

"Wow," Augustus said softly, shaking his head as he sat back down at his laptop. "She never quits."

"I wasn't aware she held the title of Town Historian," Dad responded. "That's interesting."

"I wonder what else we could find out about Ms. Longfellow?" Augustus asked as he opened his laptop.

"It's just so weird that she doesn't understand about Jesus and curses," Phoebe said as she took her seat. "When you told her back at the diner that Jesus is stronger than curses and we don't have to be afraid, she looked at you like you had three heads."

Dad gave her a gentle smile. "She hasn't been taught, Feebs," he explained. "The Bible says you shall know the truth, and the truth will set you free, but you have to *know* the truth, and you also have to believe it."

Phoebe nodded and said, "Well, one thing I know is true is that there's no sewage in that visitor's center, and those toilet explosions weren't part of any curse!"

"*Shhhhhh!*"

A frowning librarian shushed them loudly from the front desk.

Dad mouthed a silent, "*Sorry!*"

For the next hour, each of the Keens were quietly focused on their computers. Augustus and Phoebe both worked on some homeschool geography assignments, and when those were finished they turned their attention back to the Dead Nettle mystery.

Augustus opened up a messenger window and pinged Phoebe.

> A - Hey! I'm looking into Ms. Longfellow. her connection 2 all this makes me wonder. what RU up ?

> P - Exploding toilets. Finding out how somebody can make it happen without being in the room and I think I'm just about there

A few minutes later, Augustus got a message from Phoebe with a link attached.

> ***BOOM….. think I found it! put your earbuds in and watch this vid!***

Augustus watched the ten minute video with an incredulous stare. Two chemists described a highly reactive element called sodium metal. Dressed in protective gear and standing in an empty stretch of desert, the chemists threw a golf ball-sized chunk of sodium metal into a toilet, and the resulting explosion destroyed the toilet handily.

He messaged Phoebe.

> *A - You think they could have used that stuff and made it explode even though they weren't around?*

> *P - Working on that part, and I think I've got something. You can get all of this stuff from tons of places on the internet – I bet they just had it shipped straight to their house. Oooooh! I wonder if there's any way we could find the boxes it came in, like in the trash????*

Augustus grinned again and sent one more message.

> *A - Time for a dumpster dive!*

Chapter 15 – Dumpster Dive

Augustus pulled the neck of his t-shirt up over his nose as he stood beside the huge dumpster behind the visitor's center. "Oh, man, that is *rank*!" he said.

Phoebe eyed her brother's crutches. "And how do you propose to get in there and dig around with those things?" she asked.

Augustus looked down at his crutches, and then gingerly tested his pain by putting a little weight on his foot. "Oh, it's not that bad!" he said with a grin. "I'll be fine for a few minutes."

He leaned his crutches against the dumpster and hoisted himself in, carefully sliding down into the refuse. "Wish I could pinch my nose shut and go through this stuff at the same time!"

Phoebe scrambled in behind him. She stood staring open-mouthed at the garbage with her hands on her hips. "Haven't these people ever heard about recycling?" she said. "There's plastic soda bottles and cardboard mixed in with dirty diapers! And these coffee grounds and rotten apples should have been composted!" She shook her head in disbelief. "This town needs an education!"

Augustus laughed. "You're probably right, but not at this moment," he said as he started sifting through the contents. "We have a mystery to solve first."

Phoebe sighed. "I guess so," she said. "But we're almost on top of each other as it is, so why don't I get out and you toss me every cardboard box or bubble-wrap mailer thingy that looks like it could have been shipped or mailed. Then I'll dig through those and look for labels or receipts or whatever. Not sure what I'm looking for, but I'll know it when I see it."

Augustus was deeply thankful for the elbow-length rubber gloves and knee-high galoshes he was wearing. "Good plan!" he responded, nearly gagging at the pungent aroma. Careful not to put too much weight on his ankle, he added, "I gotta move the rotten food over to one corner, so give me a second and I'll just start tossing what I find."

As Phoebe clambered out and slid to the asphalt she asked, "Is this legal?"

"Yep!" Augustus said. "I double checked with Dad when I told him the plan. Dumpster diving laws are set locally, and there's no laws against it in this county or this town; we made sure."

From her vantage point behind the visitor's center, Phoebe saw a school bus go around the block toward the diner. "I wonder what people will think about us digging through the garbage!" she asked.

"Ah, who cares?" Augustus responded. "They all think we're nuts already anyway, so this will just give them more to talk about. Oh!" He fished out several cardboard boxes that were nested inside one another

84

on the top of the heap. "Heads up!" he called as he pitched the boxes over his head and out onto the ground. "I'll toss everything on this side, and you move it and look through it somewhere else so I don't hit you in the head."

Augustus held his breath and started digging through the rubbish. A cache of dirty diapers; three two-liter bottles of cream soda, all empty; six bags of moldy apples; a dozen empty beer bottles; a shredded backpack filled with oil-soaked rags; several television-sized pieces of Styrofoam; a ratty sofa cushion with half the stuffing. "Doesn't anybody use *actual* garbage bags?" Augustus asked. "I guess that makes it easier for me to ... hey! Found something else!" he said as he spied some legal-sized padded mailer envelopes leaning against the dumpster wall near the back. As he picked them up he discovered the bloated body of a dead wharf rat underneath. "Gah!" he yelled.

"What is it?" Phoebe called.

Augustus laughed. "Just an extra-large rat cooking in the sun, making it smell extra delicious down in here."

"Gross!" Phoebe responded.

It didn't take long for Augustus to dig his way to the bottom of the dumpster. He found a total of fifteen boxes of various sizes and conditions, plus eight padded mailer envelopes. Tossing the last of them to the ground, he climbed out and walked several yards away, taking in several gulps of fresh air. "My nose hairs are fried!" he said.

"You're limping," Phoebe said as she brought him the crutches.

Augustus gave her a rueful smile. "Yeah, I guess I'm not quite done with these after all."

Landon appeared just then, coming around the side of the visitor's center with a confused grin on his face. "I thought I saw you guys from the bus!" he called as he approached. "Find anything good in there?"

At that moment Phoebe stood, holding two pieces of paper in the air triumphantly, one in each hand. "Jackpot!" she announced.

"No way!" Augustus responded, coming closer to see what she was holding.

"What is it?" Landon asked. "You find money or something?"

Phoebe grinned. "Even better!" she said. "Check this out!"

She placed a four-inch square box on the ground and laid a shipping invoice on top of it and read it aloud. "Ship to: Jacob Longfellow, 601 Canyon Place, Dead Nettle, NV. From: Novus Metal Labs, 13328 East 5th St, New York, NY. Invoice for sodium metal, 1 pound volume in mineral oil 99.8%."

"No way!" Augustus repeated. "I can't believe they didn't even try to hide it!"

Landon looked back and forth between Phoebe and Augustus with a furrowed brow. "Who tried to hide what?" he asked.

Augustus looked around, scouting the roads and parking lots nearby to make sure no one was near enough to overhear them. He motioned Landon to come closer, and they all leaned their heads in together.

"Feebs, explain it to him," Augustus whispered.

"Okay, so the sodium metal is how Jacob made the toilets explode in the visitor's center," Phoebe whispered. "It's super reactive to water, and it'll explode a second or two after it gets wet. But…" She held up another piece of paper. "This little baby is how they did it without being in the building when it happened. It's the receipt for a pack of Eco-Solve dissolvable paper pouches, also shipped to Jacob Longfellow. These pouches dissolve in water in about forty seconds, and my theory is that they put a chunk of sodium metal inside these pouches and dropped them into the back of the toilet tanks and high-tailed it out of there," she explained. "They could have even doubled or tripled the pouches, giving them more time. Once the paper dissolved, the sodium metal exploded, and Jacob and Campbell were nowhere near the building at the time."

Augustus nodded excitedly. "And the sheriff made up that stupid story about there being sewage in the water. Phoebe tested it, and it was perfectly fine, but they were all up in arms and blaming *the curse*," he said, putting air quotes around the last two words. "It was straight up vandalism; we're sure of it!"

Landon's mouth dropped open. "You guys are geniuses!" he said. Then he pinched his nose shut, took two large steps backward, and grinned at Augustus. "And buddy, you *stink*!"

Phoebe laughed. "Big time! Let's toss these boxes back into the dumpster so you can go get a shower!"

Chapter 16 – The Evidence

"This must be your lucky day, Mr. Keen."

Bright and early Tuesday morning, Augustus and Phoebe had gathered up all of their evidence and joined Dad on a trip to town. Dad had called the afternoon before and set up a private meeting at the county station with Dakota Pruett, the newly hired sheriff's deputy.

"How do you mean?" Dad asked.

Deputy Pruett didn't answer right away. He was engrossed in reading the shipping receipts and water sample test results on the desk in front of him. After a few moments of silence, he gave them all a cryptic smile and said, "Why don't you come with me? I've got something to show you." He collected the envelopes and receipts and put them into an oversized manilla folder with EVIDENCE stamped across the front.

Augustus grabbed Dad's arm. "Is it really safe to leave these things here with Sheriff Longfellow around?"

The deputy stood and went to the door. "I promise on my badge that you've got nothing to worry about."

he said. "I'll personally get each item in there tagged and held in the evidence locker."

Phoebe shrugged. "These are photocopies anyway," she said with her chin in the air, looking at Deputy Pruett with a defiant stare. "So even if someone magically 'loses' them, we'll have the originals, just in case."

The deputy tipped his hat toward Phoebe with a grin and said, "My kind of sleuth!"

Deputy Pruett led the way down the hall and brought the Keen family into a room with a one-way observation window. Two familiar young men were seated at a metal table on the other side of the window, staring dejectedly at the walls.

"No way! It's the Longfellow boys!" Augustus said.

"Shhhh!" Phoebe whispered, punching Augustus in the arm. "They'll hear you!"

The deputy laughed and said, "No worries; it's soundproof. We can hear them, but they can't hear us." He gestured to a small black box on the wall to the left of the window. "You'll hear them through that speaker."

"Why are they already here?" asked Dad as he closed the door behind them.

The deputy shrugged and said, "I saw that red monster truck of theirs parked in a handicapped spot for the sixth time in a month yesterday, so I had it towed. They were caught breaking into the impound lot about three this morning, and I just had this feeling in my gut that they were somehow connected to the visitor's center explosion. And until just now, I wasn't sure exactly *how* they were connected. But the evidence you've come up with is pretty cut and dried."

They all looked up as Jacob smacked Campbell in the back of the head. "Why'd you make me park in those handicapped spots?" Jacob demanded. "Uncle Ricky's gonna kill us both!"

"Ow!" Campbell said as he rubbed the back of his head. "I didn't *make* you do anything, you dufus! That's on you! And besides, I ain't half as worried about Uncle Ricky as I am about Mama."

"You all are welcome to stay here and listen if you like," said Deputy Pruett. He left the listening booth and strode confidently into the interview room a moment later.

Augustus and Phoebe stood next to Dad, riveted to the scene unfolding on the other side of the window. Phoebe reached up and turned the volume all the way up on the speaker so they didn't miss a word.

"We know our rights!" demanded Jacob as he pounded the metal table with his fist. "Give us our phone call, *right now!*"

"You boys got a lawyer?" the deputy asked. "I strongly suggest you make that your allotted phone call, right after we're done talking."

Jacob and Campbell looked at each other with a smirk. "We don't need no lawyer," Campbell said. "Just bring our Uncle Ricky in here right quick. You'll see."

The deputy crossed his arms and said, "Well, boys, I'm afraid I can't do that, on account of the convoluted

91

mess the three of you are in together. And Sheriff Longfellow happens to be way over in Carson City all day for a training class, so he won't be back until tomorrow."

Jacob stood abruptly and moved to stand nearly nose to nose with Deputy Pruett. "I don't guess you've been around here long enough to learn how things work, Mr. Pruett," he said quietly. "You've been here, what, four months?"

The deputy didn't bat an eye. "Three. And I think I see *exactly* how things work around here," he said.

Augustus couldn't decide which of the two of them were more intimidating.

In the flash of an eye, Deputy Pruett whipped out a pair of handcuffs, spun Jacob around, and forced him to his knees. "You and your brother are under arrest for terrorism, and for the attempted murder of Conrad Bragg in connection with the explosion at the visitor's center."

Augustus was shocked at the speed with which the deputy had subdued the suspect.

Campbell's eyes went wide, all the color draining from his face. "Terrorism? Attempted murder?" He swallowed hard. "That ain't what it was!"

"Shut up, Campbell," Jacob growled as he sat back down at the table, his expression dark with fury as he stared at Deputy Pruett.

"We were just foolin' around with clippin' the fuse box, like Mama told us to," Campbell continued.

Jacob kicked Campbell hard under the table and yelled, "I said SHUT UP!"

Campbell jumped up from the table and backed up against the far wall, pointing at his brother. "Well I ain't goin' to jail for - -"

Jacob cut him off. "Think about it! Which is worse, Campbell – jail, or Mama?"

Campbell opened his mouth to reply, but no words came out. His shoulders slumped, and he sat back down in the chair and put his head in his hands.

"Why are they so afraid of their mom?" Phoebe asked.

Augustus had his phone open and was scrolling through a website when his eyes landed on a photo that made his mouth go dry. "No way!" he whispered.

Inside the interrogation room, Deputy Pruett crossed his arms and said, "Are you telling me that Harriet Longfellow put you up to this and had you vandalize the electricity *and* blow up the toilets at the visitor's center?"

Jacob smirked. "Prove it," he challenged. "We weren't anywhere near there when that explosion happened. We were getting gas up at Gilmore's, and I got a receipt."

The deputy smiled. "You're not the only one with a receipt," he said. He pulled out each piece of evidence one at a time.

The smirk slowly drained from Jacob's face as Deputy Pruett began to read aloud.

"Exhibit A: invoice for sodium metal, 1 pound volume in mineral oil 99.8%. Ship to: Jacob Longfellow, 601 Canyon Place, Dead Nettle, NV, from Novus Metal Labs, 13328 East 5th St, New York,

NY. Exhibit B: invoice for one pack of Eco-Solve Water-Soluble Pouches."

Jacob stuck his chin out and glared at the deputy. "Anybody with a printer could have left those anywhere for you to find, to try and frame us."

Deputy Pruett nodded and said, "That is true. Which is why we will subpoena Novus Metal Labs and Eco-Solve for their shipping and credit card records. I fully expect they'll both show one of the Longfellows on the credit card."

Jacob looked at his brother and growled, "I told you to get rid of those receipts, you idiot!"

Campbell's eyes went wide. "I did! I threw them away!" He stood and began to pace the length of the room, running both hands through his hair. Augustus thought Campbell was actually going to cry. "She's gonna kill us!" Campbell whispered.

Augustus leaned over to Phoebe and said, "Campbell doesn't look so good. He's all pale and shaky, and looks like he's having trouble breathing."

Phoebe nodded sadly. "Textbook panic attack, I think."

Campbell put his hand on his chest and sank to his knees on the floor. "Jacob, my chest hurts again!"

The deputy eyed Campbell with his brow furrowed in concern. "You all right, son?"

Jacob waved him off with a roll of his eyes. "My little brother has panic attacks and whenever he does, his says his chest hurts. Happens all the time, and he'll get over it."

Deputy Pruett nodded. "Campbell, you do yourself some deep, slow breathing and see if you can calm yourself down for a few minutes, okay?" he said gently.

Campbell obeyed with a nod, sucking in several long breaths and exhaling slowly with his eyes closed. After a few minutes he looked at Deputy Pruett and nodded. "Better," he said quietly.

The deputy crossed his arms and said, "Good to hear that. Now, who wants to tell me why you boys are so afraid of your mother?"

Campbell looked at his brother wide-eyed, and Jacob shook his head no.

Campbell swallowed hard, looked at Deputy Pruett, and said, "It's because she's a– ."

"Quiet!" Jacob yelled, cutting his brother off. He stood and strode purposefully to Deputy Pruett. "Phone call. *NOW*!"

Chapter 17 – The Truth

Dad led the kids back outside while Deputy Pruett was busy processing the paperwork for the Longfellow boys. Since they'd all skipped breakfast to meet the deputy early, Dad headed straight to Milly's Diner for brunch. Once the waitress had taken their order, Phoebe turned to Augustus.

"Spill it," she demanded. "You found something online back at the station, and I want to see!"

Augustus nodded and pulled his phone from his pocket. "I was scrolling through some ancestry websites, looking into the Blackwood's family tree and you won't believe what I found." He scrolled through his phone for a moment, and then held it up so Dad and Phoebe could see. "Well, first thing: I found this article about the last church in Dead Nettle closing, and it was Harriet Longfellow that made it happen. There was some kind of scandal three years ago and she sued the preacher. Even though her case was thrown out of court and it never came to anything, she dragged the preacher through the mud and he was basically forced to close the church."

Dad thoughtfully sipped his coffee. "But that wouldn't necessarily make the Longfellow boys afraid of her," he said. "And I thought you were researching Merletta Blackwood."

Augustus nodded and laid his phone on the table so they could see. "I was."

Phoebe and Dad leaned in. The website showed a photo of thirteen women all dressed in black, standing in a circle out in the desert with their hands up in the air. A much younger Harriet Longfellow was in the center, standing inside a pentagram on the ground made of small black stones.

"No way," Phoebe breathed. "She's a witch?"

Augustus nodded. "She's not just a practicing witch," he explained. "This picture is with a newspaper article about her becoming the coven leader thirty years ago." He pointed to the person to Harriet's right, a short, impossibly old woman with waist-length white hair and piercing black eyes. "The lady beside her is Cora Blackwood, Merletta Blackwood's little sister, and she was the high priestess before Ms. Longfellow was voted in."

Phoebe's jaw dropped. "No way!" she repeated softly. "And they're just out there in the open, posting photos?"

Augustus nodded. "Apparently some covens have membership and initiations and rules and bylaws and all that stuff!" he replied. "This one is called *The Coven of Capra*, and 'capra' is actually the Latin word for goat."

Dad picked up the phone and peered closely at the image, his expression a mixture of sadness and surprise. "The Bible says that a curse without cause

97

cannot alight, so I have been wondering why this town continues to suffer such misfortune. This would explain it."

Augustus offered a lopsided smile. "What does that mean in regular English?"

Just then the waitress appeared with plates of pancakes and bacon. After blessing the food, Augustus and Phoebe dug into the meal with gusto.

Dad took a bite and said, "Here's an analogy that would explain what I said a second ago. You know that game called 'Ding Dong Ditch'?"

Augustus and Phoebe looked at each other and smiled. "Yep!"

Dad continued. "You ring the doorbell and run. But some kids take it a step further by filling a paper bag with dog poop, tossing it toward the door as they ring the doorbell, and then running away. But what would happen if the door was open before the prank started?"

Phoebe wrinkled up her nose in disgust. "Gross! Dog poop would go flying into the house and if the bag pops, poop would get all over everything!"

"Exactly!" Dad said with a nod. "So in this instance, the bag of poop is like a curse, and the house can represent the town of Dead Nettle. If the door is shut, someone can toss the poop on the doorstep but it doesn't get inside and ruin the carpet. But things like sorcery, sin, rebellion, pride, and unforgiveness – these actually create an open door that would allow the poop to make it inside and negatively impact the town."

Phoebe shook her head in wonder. "Do you think the people here know about Harriet Longfellow being an actual witch?"

Augustus shrugged. "I'm not sure how much they know, but did you see how Milly reacted when Harriet first met us at the diner?"

Dad nodded. "She was clearly terrified of the woman."

"Seems like a lot of people are, including Campbell and Jacob!" Phoebe added. "They'd rather go to jail than face her? That tells you something!"

Dad put his fork down. "I think we need to pray for the Longfellow family, right here and now."

Phoebe looked at Dad with a skeptical frown. "Pray for *them*? Aren't they a lost cause?"

Dad patted her hand softly. "Feebs, we have to remember that the Bible says, '*Surely the arm of the Lord is not too short to save.*' It means he can reach everyone, and that includes the Longfellows."

They all joined hands and bowed their heads as Dad began to pray. "Jesus, we ask You to intervene in this situation. Come and trip up the plans of the enemy, and show the Longfellow family the truth of who You are. Even right now in the jail cell, we ask that You give Jacob and Campbell dreams and angelic visitations, and that You open their eyes and bombard them with truth. Soften their hearts, that they both may come to know You as Lord and Savior."

Dad paused for a moment, and then added softly, "And Lord, we ask the same for Harriet Longfellow. Reveal Yourself to her, how much You love her, and we ask for repentance and salvation for the entire family, that You would be glorified. In Jesus name, amen."

"Amen!" said Augustus and Phoebe.

Augustus took a sip of orange juice. "So what's next?" he asked. "It's like Harriet Longfellow is purposely keeping Merletta Blackwood's original curse alive."

"So it would seem," Dad said.

Phoebe frowned. "What if she won't change? Is the town just doomed to have that open door forever?"

Dad shook his head vigorously. "Absolutely not! Almighty God and a host of heavenly angels are on our side, and I have a plan for how we can help Dead Nettle close the door to the Black Opal's Curse once and for all!"

Chapter 18 – The Muster

"I'm all ears, Mr. Keen," Pastor Randolph said.

The Keen family sat in a circle with Pastor Charles Randolph in his living room. Dad had looked up an address and knocked on the door of a modest parsonage home at half past ten the next morning. The former pastor of New Life Community Church was in his late sixties with salt-and-pepper hair and pleasant laugh lines around his eyes. His wife Priscilla brought them all a glass of lemonade before she sat on the couch beside him with an expectant smile. Augustus thought she reminded him of his own Granny, and he liked her immediately.

Dad leaned forward with his hands clasped together. "The Lord keeps reminding me about the power of forgiveness," he started gently.

Pastor Randolph nodded with a sad smile. "Oh, yes. I'll admit it took some time, and I spent months wrestling with the Lord after the church was shut down. But deep in my heart I can say that I've truly forgiven Ms. Longfellow for what she did, and that I harbor no ill will against her."

Priscilla squeezed her husband's hand and added, "That goes for both of us – everything Charles just said!"

"That's wonderful to hear," Dad said. "But that's not really where I was going when I said the Lord has shown me the way to freedom for Dead Nettle."

The pastor cocked his head sideways. "I'm listening."

"Tell me what you know of Merletta Blackwood," Dad said.

Pastor Randolph rolled his eyes. "All that superstitious hooey about a curse?" he said with a wave of his hand.

Priscilla said, "I've always thought it was just an old wives' tale, people telling ghost stories around campfires to scare the kids."

"But it's real!" Phoebe insisted.

Augustus pulled out his phone and called up the photos of the creepy writing they had taken in the mine. "Take a look at what we found!"

The pastor peered closely at the screen for a second. Then he jumped up to hold the phone against a mirror in the hallway, and his expression morphed from skepticism to shock in a few seconds as he read what was written there.

"You can read Latin," Dad stated softly.

Pastor Randolph handed the phone back to Augustus and sank to the couch, his eyes wide. "I can," he managed.

Priscilla looked back and forth between Dad and Pastor Randolph. "What is it?" she asked. "What does it say?"

After a few moments of stunned silence the pastor responded. "It's a curse against the land and the people of Dead Nettle, and I won't repeat what it says." He looked up at Augustus and asked, "Where did you find this?"

"Phoebe and I found it inside the Blackwood Mine last week," Augustus replied.

"And from what we know of the timeline of the mine collapse, I believe the curse has been on that cave wall since 1917," Dad explained.

The pastor let out a long, slow breath. "I had no idea." He looked at Dad. "Merletta Blackwood gets the credit, I assume?" he asked.

Dad nodded. "That's what I believe," he said quietly. "This curse was on the wall in a section of the mine that's just a few feet from where the Billings Opal was discovered. That land, and that priceless opal, legally belonged to Ms. Blackwood. But the Billings family mined it for years without her consent. They simply stole it from her."

Pastor Randolph's jaw dropped. "You're certain?" he whispered.

Dad nodded again. "Absolutely. We confirmed it with county land records. And I think the first step in setting things right is that the town of Dead Nettle needs to come together, confess the sin, and ask for forgiveness for what the Billings family – and the whole town – did to her."

103

The pastor shook his head as he stared at the floor in shock and sadness. "I've lived here all my life, and no one's ever told me this!"

"There's more!" Phoebe added. "Gus, show Pastor Randolph the article you found about the coven."

Augustus opened a browser on his phone and found the article about the Coven of Capra. "It seems that Harriet Longfellow has followed in the Blackwood family's footsteps," he said as he handed over the phone.

Pastor Randolph took the phone and stared open-mouthed at the photo. He read the short article about the coven, and Priscilla leaned in and read it with him.

Priscilla's face went pale as she read, and she swallowed hard as she looked at Augustus. "What do you mean, *family's footsteps*?"

"Merletta Blackwood had a sister named Cora, and Cora was the high priestess of the coven before handing it over to Harriet," Dad explained.

"Oh my goodness! It's all making sense to me now!" Pastor Randolph said. "When Ms. Longfellow brought the lawsuit against me for some sort of made-up spiritual abuse accusation, I just thought she was mentally ill or maybe having an emotional breakdown. But now I see it for what it was – a spiritual battle designed to do away with Dead Nettle's only church!"

Priscilla stared at the photo of Harriet with the Coven of Capra. "So Harriet *is* a witch, then," she whispered. "It was her plan all along, to do whatever it took to shut the church down." She handed the phone back to Augustus, and added, "You're right, Charles.

Now the whole lawsuit thing *does* make sense. I kept wondering why she was so vile and manipulative, and now I see why."

Phoebe nodded vigorously. "We also found out that it was Jacob and Campbell Longfellow who cut the wires at the visitor's center on purpose so the new opal exhibit couldn't take place. Of course, Ms. Longfellow blamed it on the curse. And then the Longfellow boys got some sodium metal off the internet, along with some water soluble paper, and they're the ones that made the toilets explode. Sheriff Longfellow came into the center not even a minute after it happened and condemned the building, saying it was full of raw sewage, but he lied!"

Augustus nodded and said, "Seems like it was all done at Harriet's request, because she kept telling everyone the new opal was a fake, and didn't want the exhibit to take the spotlight off of her family. But now Jacob and Campbell are in jail charged with terrorism and attempted murder, and Sheriff Longfellow is in on it. Deputy Pruett has all the evidence."

Charles and Priscilla looked at each other open-mouthed. Then Priscilla whispered, "But how can we stop a century-old curse, much less someone like Harriet Longfellow?"

Dad rose to his feet, getting more animated as he spoke. "I truly believe God has shown me that after forgiveness, the next step is to remind the believers in this town that the word of God says, *'Greater is He who is in me than He who is in the world!'* Jesus has given us authority over every demon, and the Bible says that even satan himself is under our feet. That includes witches! Let's gather your church together, go up to that high place, and ask for God's help to break the curse!"

The pastor jumped up and hurried to his study, returning a moment later with an old fashioned Rolodex, which he handed to Priscilla. "Let's call our prayer warriors!" he said with a wide grin.

Two hours later there were six more people crowded around Pastor Randolph's tiny living room. The first of the parishioners to arrive were Tom and Tabitha Baker, the pastor's next door neighbors and former church board members. Long-time Dead Nettle residents Winifred Moon and her sister Virginia Beecham showed up next, two tiny white-haired women who were spry and full of spunk. Mail carrier James Silverman was next, followed by his sister Marla Chesterfield. Eleven people in all sat in a circle, looking to Pastor Randolph expectantly, and Augustus could feel their excitement.

Pastor Randolph stood with an open Bible in his hands, smiling broadly at everyone in the circle. "I'm so honored that you've come," he began.

A flash of lightning illuminated the early afternoon sky, followed immediately by a clap of thunder so loud that every window in the parsonage rattled as the power went out.

Phoebe reached out and grabbed Dad's hand, and he gave it a reassuring squeeze.

Pastor Randolph began to read from his Bible. *"Greater is He who is in me, than he who is in the world."*

Another flash of lightning streaked across the sky, and a mighty wind began to buffet the house. Augustus glanced out the window and saw several trees swaying violently in the yard. But his jaw dropped when he saw a copse of trees and a swing set down the street, all standing motionless.

At that moment everyone in the room nearly jumped out of their skin as Conrad Bragg burst in through the front door. Dad jumped up to help him close the door against the force of the wind.

Conrad stood by the door, disheveled and visibly shaking as his gaze went from person to person around the room. His expression waffling between confusion and fear, he finally said, "I don't know why I'm here, but … something weird is going on!"

Dad smiled and said, "Everyone, this is my friend Conrad Bragg, the owner of the Blackwood Mine." He turned to shake Mr. Bragg's hand and added, "The Holy Spirit brought you here just in time!"

Priscilla brought him an extra chair from the kitchen, and the group turned expectant eyes toward Charles Randolph.

The pastor held up his Bible and addressed the circle of believers, his eyes burning with intensity. "Friends, it's time we started acting like the word of God is true."

Chapter 19 – Into the Storm

Ignoring the howling winds, twelve people scurried from Pastor Randolph's parsonage and boarded the church's fifteen-passenger van a short while later. "She hasn't been cranked in months, so everybody pray!" the pastor said with a smile.

The van roared to life without issue, and as the pastor headed toward the main road, Priscilla turned around from the front passenger seat and said, "Let's all say the Lord's Prayer together as we drive!"

They all recited the prayer in unison, slowly and with great reverence. Augustus grinned as he saw that even Conrad Bragg had joined in.

Our Father who art in heaven,
Hallowed be Thy name.
Thy kingdom come, Thy will be done
On Earth as it is in heaven.
Give us this day our daily bread,
And forgive us our debts,
As we forgive our debtors.
Lead us not into temptation,
But deliver us from evil.
For Thine is the kingdom and the power

And the glory forever and ever. Amen.

As the van neared the Blackwood Mine, Dad turned to Conrad and said, "I'm so glad you're here!"

Conrad shook his head with a perplexed smile. "I was reading in the office at the bed and breakfast, and I guess I fell asleep in the chair, and I had this dream that was so *lifelike*! I was standing inside the old part of the mine and an angel was washing that curse off the walls, almost like pressure-washing. But instead of using water, he used this light that was so bright I couldn't look at it."

"Wow!" said Augustus. "Is that what made you come over to Pastor Randolph's house?"

Conrad's chin began to tremble, his eyes widening. "When I woke up from the dream, I stepped outside to take a walk and clear my head, and..." He glanced from Dad to Augustus. "This is going to sound nutso, but I saw this black thing, like a swarm of angry bees or something, rise up from that huge blue Victorian house at the top of the hill. As I stood there watching, it's as if that thing *noticed* me and split in two. One of the swarms came directly at me, so I just started running like a crazy man to get away from it." He shrugged. "I saw all the cars parked outside the parsonage and recognized your Mini-Cooper, and I figured you'd have some answers for me." He looked up at Dad with tears in his eyes. "I believe you now," he whispered. "I believe all of it, every word you said before about God and demons and all that." He laughed and added, "I guess I started praying while I

109

was running for my life, and I have no doubt that Jesus rescued me!"

Dad clapped Conrad on the shoulder. "That's wonderful news!"

Augustus gestured back toward town. "Did you know that big blue house belongs to Harriet Longfellow?" he asked. "And it turns out that she's actually a witch!"

Conrad shook his head slowly as realization dawned on him. "I didn't know that, but given everything that's happened up until now, it makes sense!" He gazed intently at Dad for a few moments. "What exactly is supposed to happen when we get up to the mine? Because I have no idea what I'm doing!"

Dad smiled. "I feel in my spirit that if we as a group confess the sin the Billings committed, pray for forgiveness, and renounce the curse that Merletta Blackwood cast on the town, that we will see a demonstration of God's power. That's one reason I'm sure God sent you to Pastor Randolph's house today, because you being part of this is crucial."

Conrad said, "That's all well and good, but I still don't know the right words!"

Dad nodded and said, "Don't you worry about that! I'm happy to lead you in a prayer if you aren't sure what to say, but let's see what the Holy Spirit does!"

Several minutes later the van came to a stop. Everyone looked out the windows as low clouds began to gather in the sky above the Blackwood Mine. Pastor Randolph began to quote Scripture with a passion that gave Augustus goosebumps.

110

"Have I not commanded you? Be strong and courageous! Do not be frightened, and do not be dismayed, for the LORD your God is with you wherever you go."

He turned around to face the passengers with a determined expression and said, "Let's do this together, with the power of the Holy Spirit."

Chapter 20 – Power Encounter

"Is it really only two-thirty, Dad?" Phoebe asked as they all climbed out of the van. "It's so dark!"

Dad glanced at his watch and then looked up at the sky. "Yep!" he answered.

"Those clouds are intense!" Augustus added.

"Sandstorms aren't all that unheard of in this part of the country," Phoebe said.

Dad nodded. "This is no ordinary sandstorm," he said quietly as he took Phoebe's hand. Augustus managed fairly well with his crutches and began to follow the group up the trail, Dad and Phoebe bringing up the rear. "Remember that Jesus goes before us, and he is with us," Dad said. "I'm convinced more than ever that he brought us here for such a time as this."

Just then a decades-old green sedan with a cracked windshield and rusted hood drove up the path and parked behind the church van. All three of the Keens turned around, and Phoebe stepped instinctively behind Dad when she saw Campbell Longfellow climb out of the car.

Augustus could clearly see that Campbell had been crying. Both hands were clutching his chest, and his eyes darted to-and-fro as if he feared some sort of ambush.

"No way!" Phoebe whispered.

Dad let go of Phoebe's hand and whispered, "Wait right here. Why don't the two of you pray while I chat with this guy?"

"Lord we really need you right now!" Augustus thought.

Phoebe stood behind Augustus, and he could clearly see that his sister was trembling. Remembering a verse he had memorized in church, Augustus said, *"If God is for us, who can be against us? For I am convinced that neither death nor life, neither angels nor demons, neither the present nor the future, nor any powers, neither height nor depth, nor anything else in all creation, will be able to separate us from the love of God that is in Christ Jesus our Lord.* Amen!"

Dad slowly approached Campbell with his hands up defensively. "You okay, buddy?" he asked.

The dust-laden wind was fierce, and Augustus had to wipe grit from his eyes as he strained to hear the conversation.

Campbell shook his head slowly. "I don't think so, Mr. Keen," he managed, repeatedly looking over his shoulder as his chest heaved in fear. "I was too afraid to go home after Mama posted bail, so I borrowed my friend's car and just started driving, and I swear it's like something was chasing me all over town, and I really don't know how I ended up here." He looked at Dad, his fearful expression giving way to urgent pleading. "My chest hurts so much, but when I was driving around, I kept seeing your face! It's weird, but somehow I think you can help me get away from - - "

Campbell was thrown to the ground mid-sentence by an unseen force, and he began to shake with what looked like an epileptic seizure. Augustus and Phoebe took several steps back, but held their ground as Augustus said, "Jesus we need you! Come, Holy Spirit!" He looked up at the sky as it grew darker by the minute.

Dad knelt in the rocky dirt and put his hand on Campbell's chest, ignoring the boy's writhing as well as the swirling sand. "In the name of Jesus, I bind you, evil spirit, and I cast you into the pit!" Dad said loudly. "By the power of the resurrected Christ, I command you to leave this man's body!"

Campbell rolled over onto his side and coughed violently three times, then became still. Augustus watched open-mouthed as Campbell pulled himself up into a seated position and looked at Dad in astonishment, both hands on his chest.

"It's gone!" he said, his eyes wide with wonder. "It's been inside me, this pressure right here in my chest for years, and I felt it leave!"

Dad nodded and said, "Praise God! But there's some business we need to do in order for the demon to stay gone, because if we don't take care of something right here and now, that demon has every right to come back and torment you, or worse. Are you ready to surrender your life to Jesus?"

Campbell nodded as tears began to flow down his cheeks. "I'll do anything!"

114

Augustus could hardly keep back his own tears as he watched Dad lead Campbell Longfellow in a prayer of salvation. A minute later, Dad helped Campbell to his feet, and the two embraced as Campbell wept openly.

Augustus glanced at his sister and saw that she was holding back tears of her own. "I never would have expected that!" she managed.

From behind him, Augustus heard Conrad Bragg's voice. "And neither would I!" he said. Augustus and Phoebe turned and realized the group had been behind them the whole time and had witnessed it all. Every one of them was grinning or clapping or crying with joy.

Pastor Randolph strode forward with his arms wide open, a tearful smile on his face. "May God be praised, and all the angels in heaven rejoice!" he said as he enveloped Campbell in a bear hug.

Dad raised his eyes to the top of the trail where the silhouette of the Blackwood Mine was illuminated by several flashes of lightning. "Now let's get up there and finish what we came here to do!"

Campbell shook his head and took a step back. "But we can't!" he protested.

Dad put his arm around Campbell's shoulders and steered him gently toward the trail as the rest of the group fell into step behind them. "The Bible tells us we have authority over every evil spirit, son. With Jesus on our side, we have absolutely *nothing* to fear." He leaned closer to Campbell as he added firmly, "And that includes an entire coven of witches."

Campbell's jaw dropped. "You know about that?" he asked as he walked.

Dad nodded. "The Bible also says, '*For nothing is secret that will not be revealed, nor anything hidden that will not be known and come to light*.' And as God reveals the enemy's plans, we can take authority over every last demon and kick them out!"

The group was buffeted by harassing winds that seemed to increase in strength the closer they came to the mine, and Augustus's crutches made his trek that much more challenging. Once they were all assembled at the Blackwood Mine ten minutes later, Dad brought Campbell to the front. The two of them knelt in the dirt, a few feet from the rubble of the collapsed mine entrance. He motioned for Pastor Campbell and Conrad Bragg to join them.

The rest of the group circled around behind them, and several lifted their hands and began to pray or sing quietly. Everyone had to shield their eyes against the grit-filled wind.

"Father God, Your word says that wherever two or more are gathered in Your name, You are there in the midst of them," Dad began. "We come to you in humble surrender today, and ask for Your power, Your wisdom, and Your guidance now in Jesus name."

Augustus looked around, and he felt his flagging courage rise up as he looked at the faith-filled expressions of the praying men and women around them.

Dad turned to Campbell and said, "The Billings and the Longfellows stole a priceless fiery opal from

Merletta Blackwood over a century ago, and we need to confess that and ask for forgiveness. Will you tell God what's on your heart? It doesn't need to be big words or anything fancy. Just be honest."

Campbell swallowed hard and nodded, then looked up at the sky and began to pray. "God, I'm not real good with words and stuff, but it's me, Campbell Edward Longfellow! And my family did something really awful all those years ago, and I'm here to say I'm sorry for what they did to that lady!"

Lightning flashed overhead several times, but Campbell continued, becoming more emotional with every word. "God, please forgive my family and the Billings family, and I'm asking You to erase that terrible thievery and make it like it never happened. And Miss Merletta Blackwood, I guess you probably can't hear me right now, but I'm so, *so* sorry that my family stole from you, and I ask for forgiveness for what they did to you, and how they all treated you so bad back then!"

Augustus saw the effects of the wind as three small dirt devils swirled violently around the group. But he realized with a start that the sand spouts seemed to be repelled by a barrier he couldn't see. He smiled as a Bible verse came to his mind, and he spoke it aloud, even if only to encourage himself. *"The angel of the Lord encamps around those who fear him, and he delivers them."*

Dad clapped Campbell on the back and said, "Amen! Well done, young man!" Then he turned to Conrad and said, "Remember when I said that

117

ownership is a powerful thing? You have authority over this land that you own, and you have all authority to break any curse that was spoken over it, because Jesus gave you that authority! It's time to renounce the curse, Conrad."

Conrad bowed his head, and Augustus could see the wiry miner's shoulders shaking. "Jesus!" he shouted. "We come together, the residents of Dead Nettle and me as the owner of this land that You created. We renounce any curse spoken over this land and this town. We claim this land for God, and command every word of that curse to be washed away by the powerful light of God, just like You showed me! In Jesus name, amen!"

Dad stood to his feet and raised his arms overhead, praying in a loud voice. "Now Lord, because of Your people's prayers of forgiveness, as Your representative and invited guest here, I break every curse that has been over this town and these people. I revoke those curses now, in the name of Jesus Christ the Son of God. In His all-powerful name, I declare the town of Dead Nettle and its residents released from every curse. Satan, I declare to you that you have no more claims here, that you have no more access to Dead Nettle, to the residents, or to their families, and you have no more access to their businesses or their finances. These people have been lifted out of the domain of darkness and welcomed into the kingdom of the Son of God's love. Thank You, Jesus! Amen!"

The whirling sand spouts collapsed in on themselves, scattering dust and pebbles in the dirt as they came to nothing.

The clouds above the Blackwood Mine parted in the middle and scattered, and a strong afternoon sun caused everyone to shield their eyes, blinking in the sudden brightness. One by one, every person offered up quiet prayers of praise and thanksgiving.

The winds died down, and in seconds a fresh, moisture-laden breeze began to blow, bringing the unmistakable promise of rain.

Confused and thrilled at the same time, Conrad and Campbell shook hands with one another, and then embraced each other heartily, with good-natured claps on the back.

Phoebe raced to hug Dad, and Augustus joined in with a group hug as Dad kissed the tops of their heads. "That was amazing!" Augustus said.

Pastor Randolph cleared his throat and loudly addressed the group with a tearful grin. "I'm here to announce that The New Life Community Church is officially reopening as of right now!"

Chapter 21 – The End of the Matter

"It hardly even looks like the same place!" Augustus said as they drove into Dead Nettle on a beautiful Saturday morning in September.

Only six months had elapsed since the encounter at the Blackwood Mine, but Augustus could scarcely believe the change that had come over the once dilapidated town.

"Mom, when we were here in March, all the yards looked _so_ different!" Phoebe said. "I remember there used to be a burned out gas station right there, but now it's a cute little roadside fruit stand!"

Augustus pointed to several of the yards as they drove by. "Remember how brown and sad everything looked before?" he asked. "I guess the drought is over!"

Dad smiled and said, "In more ways than one!"

As they drew closer to the KOA, Augustus grinned when he saw the town's refurbished welcome sign. "Check it out, Mom! Someone had painted graffiti on it last time we were here, and now it's brand new!"

"_Welcome to Dead Nettle: a Lively Town_," Mom read. "From what I've seen so far, this hardly looks at all like the place you described."

Dad chuckled and said, "The change is really remarkable!"

They set up the RV at the campground in the same site they'd chosen last spring, and they were just about finished getting the Mini-Cooper unhooked when a familiar voice called to Augustus from the pool.

"Yo, Gus! You made it!" Landon called as he sprinted in their direction.

"Landon!" Augustus said with a wide grin. "Mom, this is Landon, the guy I told you about that we met here last time, the one I've been texting a bunch."

Mom stuck her hand out and said, "Glad to meet you, Landon. I'm Candace Keen."

Landon shook Mom's hand and then turned to Augustus, antsy with excitement. "I didn't want to tell you over a text message, but guess what?! Grandma and I got an actual apartment in town last month! We don't have to live in the camper anymore!"

Phoebe cheered as Augustus gave Landon a high five. "That's awesome!" he said.

Dad clapped Landon on the shoulder. "That's great news, kiddo!" Then Dad knelt down so he could look Landon in the eye. "Augustus shared your messages with me about both you and your grandmother accepting Jesus a couple months ago, too, and how you're both involved in the New Life Community Church. That's the best news of all!"

Landon smiled and looked at the ground. "Well after everything that happened back in March, it was pretty hard to just sweep it all under the rug, you know?" he said. He gestured toward the town and added, "And you guys are not gonna *believe* how different it is here now. I hardly believe it myself!" He gave Phoebe a rueful smile and said, "It's like you said last spring. You can't see the wind, but you can see what the wind does, and that God is like that. Well, everybody can see the changes around here, clear as day!"

"Truman, what time does the exhibition start?" Mom asked. "We don't want to be late!"

Dad checked his watch and said, "It starts at one, so we have time to take you to Milly's in town for some lunch beforehand. Landon, want to join us?"

He gestured over his shoulder and said, "Nah, I'm here with my friends for a little while longer, but I'll see you at the visitor's center!"

A short while later the Keen family was shown to a table at Milly's Diner, and Milly approached the table, practically beaming. "How good to see you all again!" she said with a warm smile. Reaching out her hand toward Mom she said, "I'm Milly."

After she took their orders and left the table, Augustus said to Mom, "That's Landon's grandma."

"She looks so different!" Phoebe whispered. "There's no more dark circles under her eyes, and she looks way happier than I remember!"

Dad smiled. "When the Holy Spirit changes us on the inside, it's evident on the outside!"

After a meal of burgers, fries, and warm apple pie, the Keens headed across the street to the visitor's center. The parking lot was set up with an enormous canopy tent, inside which were dozens of chairs and

122

two long tables laden with trays of sweets and goodies of all kinds. A line of people snaked around the building, even though the exhibition didn't start for another forty-five minutes.

Augustus recognized the sheriff's deputy standing by the door.

"Deputy Pruett!" Dad said with his hand out. "Great to see you again! This is my wife Candace, and I'm sure you remember Augustus Blue and Phoebe."

The deputy returned Dad's handshake and said, "Of course! Good to have you all back again. And actually, it's *Sheriff* Pruett now," he added, tapping on his badge. "Seems I had a little promotion back in April, and I have you all to thank for it!"

Phoebe grinned. "That's awesome!"

"Congratulations!" Dad said.

Augustus was about to burst with curiosity. "So what happened with Sheriff Longfellow?"

Phoebe said, "And the rest of the Longfellows? Are they all still here?"

The Sheriff shook his head. "So after the truth came to light back in March, the county was all set to press legal charges against the four of them for vandalism, terrorism, criminal conspiracy – a whole slew of things. But three days before their initial court date the first week of April, Jacob, Harriet, and Ricky disappeared in the middle of the night. They didn't take a single thing with them from the house, it seems; not an extra change of clothes, a jacket, or even Ms. Longfellow's Cadillac. It's like they just fell off the map."

Augustus and Phoebe looked at each other open-mouthed.

"What about Campbell?" Augustus asked.

The sheriff shook his head. "Campbell had been staying with Charles Randolph and his wife, because he didn't feel safe going back to his mother's house after that night in jail. Poor kid was as shocked as all of us when he found out his family disappeared. But he's had the most remarkable life turn-around of anyone I've ever seen! He even drives the church bus on Sundays!"

"That's great to hear!" Dad said with a tender smile.

Sheriff Pruett continued. "Campbell took a plea deal and was sentenced to a boatload of community service. He's been busting his tail week in and week out all summer long, helping people rebuild broken down buildings and repaint. He's actually got a real knack for it!" The sheriff offered a broad smile. "The change in him is nothing short of miraculous!"

Dad nodded and said, "Oh, I can believe it!"

"What about their big blue house on the hill?" Augustus asked. "Does Campbell still live there?"

Sheriff Pruett shook his head with a rueful smile. "Apparently Ms. Longfellow hadn't paid taxes on that house for ten years, so the county put it up for auction. A big family with a whole mess of kids bought it for the back taxes, which is likely a tenth of what it's worth. And that's only the beginning of all the changes around here!" the sheriff said. He took a deep breath and looked up at the sky. "It's as if the air itself is lighter now, easier to breathe," he said. "Almost immediately after the Longfellows left, and after you did … whatever it was that you did up at the mine, it's like the town was nearly reborn."

Augustus and Phoebe each looked at each other with a smile as Dad said, "I think that's a perfect way to describe it, Sheriff!"

The sheriff glanced at his watch and then opened the visitor's center door. "Mr. Bragg said you're all on the guest list, so you can come on inside. He was asking about you earlier." He tipped his hat toward them with a smile. "Nice to see you all again, and nice to meet you, Mrs. Keen!"

The visitor's center had been transformed into an elegant exhibition hall, with fresh paint, soft lighting, modern display cases, and eye-catching artwork paying tribute to the beauty of the local gemstones and the bygone era of mining. And Augustus grinned as he saw the doors to a newly reconstructed bathroom, with no trace of the prior explosion and flooding to be seen anywhere.

~ ~ ~

The next morning, the Keens had said their goodbyes to all of their friends and piled into the old Winnebago. Mom rode shotgun, and a huge paper map was open in her lap as Dad buckled his seatbelt. As was his custom before starting out on any road trip, he bowed his head and began to pray.

"Lord, we are so thankful for what You have done here in this town! Thank You, Holy Spirit, for the transformed lives that can only come from Your resurrection power. You are such a good Father!" he said.

"And God," Augustus chimed in, "bless Landon and his grandma!"

"Yes," Dad responded. "Lord bless them, and Mr. Bragg, and Pastor Randolph and his church, and Sheriff Pruett, and Campbell Longfellow. Keep them, protect them, send Your angels to encamp around them. May Your face shine upon them and give them peace. In Jesus' name, Amen."

"Amen!" everyone echoed.

Dad cranked up the RV. As they pulled out of the KOA, Augustus Blue leaned forward with an expectant smile.

"Where to next, Dad?"

THE END

Acknowledgements

To the real Augustus Blue – thank you for having such a sleuth-worthy moniker! I hope you love the character that bears your name.

To Liz Bowlin – thank you for being my biggest fan, and for being such a wonderful friend.

To the Magdich family – thank you for being beta readers, and for being my perfect target audience!

To Chad – I love you immensely! I'm so honored to have your lifelong support of my writing.

To Dad – thank you for the inspiration to write this series!

To Nanci – thank you for ALLLLLLL the feedback and input and the plethora of story ideas! Love you, twinkie swisser!

Thank you most of all to my Lord and Savior Jesus Christ. My prayer is that all of my writing points to You, and You only.

About the Author

A.S. Mackey's lifelong love for reading and creative writing was solidified with a Bachelor's Degree in English Literature from the University of Georgia in 1991. She has written multiple children's stories on a contract basis with Tiny Readers Publishing in Houston (the *Zack and Katie* series), and she has authored several non-fiction/educational books for young ESL readers with Norwegian publisher Sigbjörn Dugal.

Her debut middle grade fiction novel *The Edge of Everywhen* was published by B&H Publishing/Lifeway in May of 2020. The novel won the SCWC Notable Book Award in 2021 and was a finalist in the 2021 ACFW Carol Awards in the debut category.

Mrs. Mackey is a published and listed member of the Society of Children's Book Writers and Illustrators (SCBWI), and is also a member of the American Christian Fiction Writers (ACFW). She served as a faculty consultant with the Alabama Writing Workshop in 2019, and has conducted many author talks in schools and libraries around the southeast. She currently makes her home in Florence, Alabama where she and her husband Chad are worship leaders and church planters with the Vineyard. She has three adult children, a son-in-law, a daughter-in-law, and a cat named Penelope.

Find A.S. Mackey online at www.asmackey.com, and the author would be stoked if you'd leave a thoughtful review on Amazon!

Made in the USA
Columbia, SC
13 September 2023

22834879R00076